The Emerald Slippers of Oz

D1082232

The Emerald Slippers of Oz

The Emerald Slippers of Oz

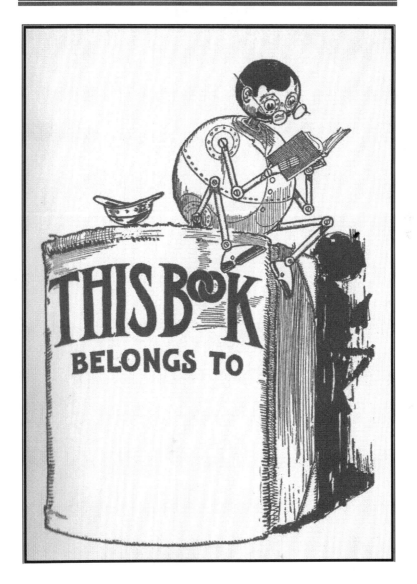

The Emerald Slippers of Oz

by

James C. Wallace II
Amanda D. Wallace

Royal Liaison of Oz
Royal Liaison to Princess Ozma

Founded on and continuing the famous Oz stories
by *L. Frank Baum*

Scientia Est Vox Press
2013

8

The Emerald Slippers of Oz

This story is dedicated to our
beloved granddaughter;
Heavenlee Angel Skie Johns,
whose brief but wonderful time in
our lives will never be forgotton.

List of Chapters

Chapter One
Dorothy Ponders A Gift

The sun set slowly over Emerald City on the evening of Princess Ozma's Grand Celebration of Her Birthday, which just so happened to be on August twenty first. It had been a glorious celebration, attended by nearly everyone in Emerald City and many folks from the surrounding countryside. There were Munchkins and Winkies and Quadlings... Oh my, I almost forgot the Gillikins, who were also in attendance. There was much gaiety and joy, punctuated by music, food and laughter and all things wonderful where Princess Ozma was concerned.

Her Majesty had ruled over Oz for more years than anyone could remember and during all that time, no harm had ever befallen anyone in Oz, though it could have been argued by the likes of the now-deceased Wicked Witches of the East and West. Still though, Her reign was calm and peaceful, marked only by the occasional misadventures that often come when people are bored... or unhappy, a condition which Princess Ozma endeavored to alleviate whenever necessary.

Dorothy Gale, of Kansas, sat near the large throne which dominated the central Grand Throne Room of Princess Ozma's Royal Palace. She pondered the day's events, smiling every now and then at the thought of the Scarecrow, attempting to dance and generally making quite a silly show of it, or of the Tin Woodman, clanking about and spreading much joy and laughter at his equally silly antics. Even the Cowardly Lion had gotten into the act as He granted the occasional request for a loud roar during the day's festivities.

Overall, the party had gone well and Dorothy was pleased another year in Oz had passed peacefully under Princess Ozma's reign. Dorothy had lived in Oz now for many years, along with Aunt Em and Uncle Henry, and she had found great joy in her life among the citizens of Oz.

The next day, the little girl from Kansas began considering next year's celebration. She talked to her good friend, Billina the Hen about this and pondered what she might give her good friend, Princess Ozma as a birthday present.

She explained to the hen how every year, she always gave her friend the same gift; a simple silk dress of pearly white, accented with small emeralds and rubies, as well as the occasional amethyst, blue topaz and yellow sapphire gems.

Every year, Princess Ozma accepted graciously and would wear the dress upon occasion throughout the year.

14

The Emerald Slippers of Oz

It had become almost routine and Dorothy, who had been declared a princess herself many years ago, decided that "next year would be different!"

The Emerald Slippers of Oz

For six months, Dorothy pondered the idea of a new gift for Princess Ozma. The Royal Monarch had just about everything imaginable under the Ozian sun and Dorothy became frustrated at not being able to think of a single thing that might make a fine birthday gift. It occasionally showed and Princess Ozma thought to ask Her good friend what was upon her mind, but decided not to as She knew Dorothy well and was certain Dorothy would solve her dilemma in her own good time.

About one month or so before the Vernal Equinox, a holiday which signaled the approach of Spring and which Princess Ozma loved dearly, Dorothy happened upon a pair of white leather slippers in the palace hall. She knew these to belong to Princess Ozma and Dorothy held them in her hands, looking them over and marveling at how simple and yet regal they were.

"It seems silly for the Ruler of Oz to wear such simple shoes," she thought to herself as she replaced the slippers where she had found them.

All that day, the thought of the simple slippers of white leather danced through her thoughts and soon, Dorothy was struck with a wonderful idea.

"Why not present Her with a pair of emerald slippers, made with emeralds from the Emerald City itself?" she pondered out loud. "Surely She deserves better shoes than those simple ones of white leather?"

By the next morning, Dorothy was convinced that a new pair of Emerald Slippers was just the right gift for her dearest friend in all of Oz.

Chapter Two
Blinkie; the Former Witch

The forest was dark but the ugly old woman was not afraid. Not Blinkie. She wasn't afraid of anything or of anyone. Kicking at a stick that she had tripped over, Blinkie mumbled to herself about losing her magical powers so long ago.

"Someday," she thought to herself, *"I will have my powers back and then all will fear me once more!"*

She felt the black eye patch covering her left eye and wished for younger days when she still had her magical powers.

Crossing the little stream in the clearing, Blinkie looked for a certain cave where she often went when her moods were dark and foul. How cool it felt to her old bones.

Within the cave was a large flat stone that held a smooth rock about the size of a small rabbit that she used to grind the plants, roots and others flora down to a fine powder.

In her small black bag, the ugly old woman

17

withdrew several roots that she had found along the way and began grinding them to powder.

Blinkie had often done this in a desperate attempt to recreate the powders and potions of her youth, though not just any powder or potions, but magical ones that she might use once more. Though Blinkie had been deprived of her witchly powers long ago by the Scarecrow, she still longed to practice her dark and ancient arts.

Laughing wildly to herself, the ugly old woman thought how nice it would be to make herself pretty and young once more... and to have two eyes as before. She continued her grinding with even more fervor.

"*Yes,*" she thought to herself, "*then I could fool them all and make them pay dearly!*" Tears rolled down her old and wrinkled face as she laughed and laughed... and laughed.

Chapter 3
Dorothy Seeks A Shoemaker

D orothy roamed the streets of Emerald City
for several days, speaking to the locals,
most of whom she had met before over the
years. Of course, everyone she encountered knew who she
was.

Long ago, she had been declared Princess Dorothy
by Her Majesty; Princess Ozma. Dorothy, of course, was
always hesitant to use the title of Princess, having been
raised in simple, mid-western American Kansas.

"There be no royalty where I come from," she often
explained to those who fussed and fidgeted when in her
presence. "I'm just a plain 'ol farm girl from a plain 'ol
place called Kansas." She never could get used to the idea
of being royal and such.

PRINCESS
DOROTHY

Near the south end of Emerald City were the artisans who made and traded in various wares, including clothing... and of course, shoes. The plain 'ol farm girl from Kansas made inquires to several Quadling artisans who were well known for their skill with leather and cloth and

21

sole and heel.

No one seemed willing or able to accommodate Dorothy's wishes for a pair of Emerald Slippers, and all were sworn to silence," 'lest Princess Ozma find out about Her upcoming birthday present," she had told each one.

In all honesty, none felt worthy of Princess Dorothy's vision. Everyone she spoke to seemed amazed no one had ever thought of it before.

Finally, near the Lion's Gate which lies on the northern edge of Emerald City and is the primary gate through which all of the animals of Oz preferred entering or leaving, Dorothy spoke with a merchant she knew well from Gillikin Country.

"Won't you please help me in my quest for a shoemaker?" Dorothy pleaded. "No one else seems able or willing to do so."

"I can understand why," he replied. "For anyone else, any of us could do the job. But for Princess Ozma..."

Dorothy could tell that he was quite nervous about the Royal Monarch of Oz. Everyone in Emerald City loved Princess Ozma, who had long ago proven to be a kind and just Ruler, but She was a Fairy Princess... and a Fairy Princess was magical. Dorothy was merely a normal Princess.

It was a rare person in Oz who either could perform magic, or even wanted to. Magic was looked upon as something very special that only a rare few were permitted to perform. Making the Emerald Slippers for Her Majesty seemed like magic to everyone Princess

The Emerald Slippers of Oz

Dorothy spoke to.

"If only Ugu the Shoemaker were still around," The merchant pondered out loud. "He could have done it!"

Dorothy thanked the merchant and made her way back to the Royal Palace at the center of Emerald City.

The words of the merchant rolled over and over in her mind's eye as she recalled the old shoemaker and how he had tried to conquer Oz long ago.

The old shoemaker named Ugu had come from an ancient line of magicians, though he had fallen into the ways of a cobbler early in his life. Finding his ancestors magical books and instruments, he had set up shop and secretly practiced magic. Unfortunately, the power of magic corrupted him and he set about stealing the Magic Dishpan, which belonged to a Yip named Cayke the Cookie Cook. It was his intention to conquer all of Oz and be "the greatest magician in Oz!"

Soon, using the Magic Dishpan, he had stolen the Great Book of Records from Glinda and the Magic Picture from Princess Ozma. Before long, he had kidnapped the Royal Sovereign of Oz, Princess Ozma and transformed Her into a golden peach pit. In time, even the bag of the Wizard of Oz and all its magical contents were his to use.

It was only after Dorothy had found the Magic Belt and transformed Ugu into a grey dove did he cease his magical ways.

She recalled that she had forgiven him for his wickedness when he had confessed remorse, but Ugu the Shoemaker had requested to remain a dove rather than be transformed back into a citizen of the western Winkie Country of Oz, " 'lest I be tempted once more to perform magic."

The Emerald Slippers of Oz

"I wonder if Time has tempered Ugu and made him more willing to return to his old cobbler ways?" Dorothy thought to herself. *"Certainly he would make the Emerald Slippers if I asked him to?"*

The next morning found Dorothy well on her way to the western Winkie Country where her friend, the Tin Woodman ruled from his magnificent Tin Palace. She kept thinking about Ugu the Shoemaker and the power of magic.

"Perhaps the Tin Woodman will know where Ugu the Grey Dove has built his nest?" she said out loud, though no one else was in sight on the smooth stone pathway leading west across the green fields surrounding Emerald City.

Chapter 4
'Ol Mombi; The
Former Sorceress

The four-horned cow looked nervously at the old woman, then over at the pigs. Even they knew better to stay out of her way. They had learned how to tell her moods by the way she walked, the way she looked at them and even how she milked the cow.

She sat on the old wooden milking stool with her hands resting on her knees. Looking at the hay scattered about on the barn floor, 'Ol Mombi thought back to her younger days when she was known just as Mombi and had made magic and recalled well the joy it brought her. The four-horned cow and the pigs had seen that look many times as 'Ol Mombi had spent countless days reflecting on her past with bitter remorse.

She slowly got up and walked towards the house, but tripped over a root that had been exposed from her countless journeys to and from the barn.

"If only that were a root of magical origin," the old woman thought to herself. *"I could brew me up a fine potion."* 'Ol Mombi pondered the exposed root as she made her

way into the house. *"After all these years, I wonder if I could even remember how..."*

She put the pail of milk down on the table and set about preparing her morning meal. Her thoughts, once more, were focused on the past and her former glory as Sorceress of Evil

"Those were the days when a witch or a sorceress could have some fun," she cackled out loud. Her voice echoed through the empty rooms. "Oh to be able to cast a spell again, or brew up an Evil potion... just for the joy of it!"

A faint memory of Jack Pumpkinhead flashed through her mind's eye and she cackled with laughter once more.

'Ol Mombi recalled how she had obtained a small vial of the Powder of Life from Dr. Pipt, the Crooked Magician from the Munchkin Country, and had used it to bring the strange looking thing of wood and cloth and rope and pumpkin to Life. She remembered how much joy it had given her to actually bring something lifeless to Life, a feat which few in Oz had ever done.

"I will do so once again... someday soon," she thought to herself. *"Real soon..."*

Chapter 5
The Munchkin Winkies

Dorothy made good time on the polished marble road that led into Winkie Country and on towards the Tin Palace of the Tin Woodman, who ruled over the Winkies which lived there. It was not as smooth as the road of yellow brick that joined Munchkin City with the Emerald City, however, it served its purpose well.

The plain 'ol farm girl often enjoyed walking about throughout Oz. "It's much more pleasant to smell the flowers and hear the bees buzz in the nearby meadows," she mentioned once to the Tin Woodman, who had trouble understanding why she "did not take advantage of the Large Red Wagon and the Sawhorse?"

"Besides," Dorothy continued, "I get to meet and greet so many wonderful people of Oz."

Now, the smooth marble lead the Princess of Oz on towards the very shiny home of the Tin Woodman, who was known by his family name of Nick Chopper. Normally, she would have reached it in a day, but today's journey was more of a leisurely stroll.

All around her was the dominant color of yellow, being reflected in the trees, grasses and what few farmhouses, grain mills and barns she came across during her journey.

About an hour or so before sunset, Dorothy came across a farmer's home along the way. It was, of course, nearly all yellow, from the roof tiles and clapboard siding all the way down to the yellow pine picket fencing that surrounded the place.

She had stayed here before and the owners were a petite man of about fifty years old, along with his equally petite wife, both of whom were Munchkins. They were dressed in various layers of yellow fabric, which is favored in Winkie Country, although upon each was a small splash of blue from their own Munchkin Country. They gladly offered their hospitality to the Princess of Oz.

The Munchkin couple had emigrated from Munchkin Country long ago and had been there in person when Dorothy's house fell upon the Wicked Witch of the East, killing her and freeing the Munchkins from their bondage to the old woman of Evil.

"Princess Dorothy!!!" they exclaimed together, their excitement uncontained as they emerged from their home upon her approach. "It is so wonderful to invite you into our home once more!"

Dorothy blushed deeply and politely accepted their expected invitation. "Please call me Dorothy, if you can," she begged her hosts.

"Only when we're indoors, Your Royal Highness..." they both intoned as they bowed deeply before the plain 'ol farm girl from plain 'ol Kansas.

There was a small portion of laughter as all three friends saw the funniness of what they were doing.

"Where's Toto?" asked the farmer's wife. She had a fondness for the little dog of smooth black fur.

The Emerald Slippers of Oz

"He's visiting the Cowardly Lion in up in Gillikin Country," Dorothy replied. "It's the big cat's birthday and Toto didn't wanna miss all the fun."

Normally, Dorothy would attend the Cowardly Lion's birthday celebration, but recently, the big cat had decided that every other year, He would celebrate with only His subjects, the animals of Oz. This happened to be one of those years.

The famer and his wife invited Dorothy inside and before long, the farmer's wife had a fine meal prepared and served. Soon, they settled in for the evening and before long, Dorothy was sound asleep and dreaming of Emerald Slippers.

Chapter 6
The Pepperspice Stew

B linkie stood by the fireplace and stirred the stew that she cooked in her large iron kettle. She was so lost in thought that she nearly burned her supper. The old woman started mumbling to herself about her daydreams.

The roots that she had ground two days ago didn't seem to make any of the sort of magic she so desperately wanted. In fact, it made no magic at all.

Blinkie couldn't wait to get back to the nearby forest where she could find all manner of natural ingredients.

"There has to be way to find the right plants and roots around here," she thought to herself, *"but try as I may, I can't seem to find them."*

The old woman paced back and forth in front of the kettle, and her supper, mumbling to herself.

"I wonder if that pesky Scarecrow removed all the good plants and roots that witches like me love to use?" she mused silently. *"Maybe that antidote he gave me did more than return me to my normal size?"*

Her pacing grew faster and faster as she thought more and more about her encounter with the Scarecrow long ago.

The Emerald Slippers of Oz

It had been the Scarecrow that had forced Blinkie to undo all the Evil deeds she had committed during her time of magic. He had sprinkled a shrinking powder on the old witch, causing her to begin shrinking.

The Scarecrow only restored her to full height when she had fulfilled his demands that all her wrongs had been undone.

Of course, there was more to the antidote than the Scarecrow would admit to Blinkie. It had not only restored the old witch to her normal size, it had also deprived her of her magic powers.

"It must have made me forget something..." the old woman spoke out loud, "but what, I can't recall."

Blinkie stopped and looked down at her kettle.

"No," she thought to herself. *"That couldn't have*

happened."

     She must have had this conversation with herself more times than there are Munchkins in all of Oz. And as always, she could not remember her former ways of witchcraft and sorcery, despite her best efforts.

     The old woman carefully dipped out a bowl of stew for herself and sat down in the old worn wooden chair by one of the large windows which surrounded the center room of her eight-sided house.

     She sipped on a steaming hot spoonful and smiled to herself.

     "Much better than usual," she spoke out clearly, almost expecting an answer from one of the other windows. "A dash from that old box of Pepperspice was just what this old recipe needed."

     Blinkie recalled how she had found the old Pepperspice box hidden away in the farthest corner of the highest cabinet in her old kitchen just that morning. She couldn't remember when she had last looked up in that far away place.

     The Pepperspice was a welcome addition to her usual stew, which she had cooked nearly every day for as long as she could remember.

     Now, the former witch who had once ruled over all the witches in Jinxland, a place located in the southern and eastern most part of Oz, pondered once more as she slowly enjoyed her supper.

     "I wonder if I should start looking elsewhere for my needs," she mused out loud. Then, the old had another thought which she had never had before.

In a flash, she began laughing to herself. Since no one was around to hear her, the cackle of laughter echoed throughout the eight-sided house, bouncing off the surrounding glass.

Once she had regained her composure, Blinkie, the former witch spelled out her plan to no one but herself.

"I will travel all across Jinxland and even across all of Oz if that's what it takes!" she declared to the empty room. The echoes from all eight windows blended together until all she could hear was the faint echoed whisper of "...Oz..."

Suddenly, another thought crossed the old woman's mind.

"Why, I could join forces with another witch... or even a magician," Blinkie spoke softly. She looked around to make sure no one had heard her.

Several spoonfuls of stew later, she continued her ponderings.

"But who else knows as much as I do about magic?" she thought to herself. *"Well, maybe almost as much as I do."*

Chapter 7
Memories of Dr. Pipt

In the southern part of Munchkin Country, there is a small range of mountains surround by a grim and dark forest. Within those mountains lived Dr. Pipt and his wife; Margolotte. Dr. Pipt looked pleasing and plain, being a simple Munchkin gardener now. His wife, Margolotte was equally pleasant and a wonderful Munchkin cook with all the things they grew in their little blue garden.

Long ago, Dr. Pipt was known as the Crooked Magician. He was called this for two reasons. He had arms and legs so crooked that he could use all four limbs with equal dexterity, a thing which came in quite handy when he would make the Powder of Life, a powder so powerful that it could bring to Life anything it was sprinkled on. His talents also permitted him to create the Liquid of Petrifaction, a liquid which turned living creatures instantly to marble. Creating these magical potions made Dr. Pipt a powerful magician, which was the second reason why he was called the Crooked Magician.

Even though Dr. Pipt had never used his magical talents for anything but good, when his Liquid of Petrifaction had accidentally spilled on his wife,

The Emerald Slippers of Oz

Margolotte and his friend, Unc Nunkie, turning them to marble, his magical endeavors were revealed.

Princess Ozma had forbidden all but Herself, Glinda; Good Witch of the South and the Wizard of Oz; O. Z. Diggs, who had returned from the Great Outside after he was deposed as the Ruler of Oz by Princess Ozma, from practicing magic, so it was left to the Wizard to restore Margolotte and Unc Nunkie to Life and straighten up Dr. Pipt's crooked limbs so that he may never again produce any powders or liquids of magical prowess.

Now, the kindly-looking Munchkin named Dr. Pipt puttered about in his domed workshop as a small fire burned in the nearby fireplace. Through the windows which circled the hall, he saw the blue gravel paths leading to his garden and around the grounds. The blue of cabbage and carrot that stood out among the numerous blue vegetables growing there pleased him greatly.

"You hungry, dear?" asked Margolotte as she entered the circular hall. "I'm gathering some blue butter from the buttercups, so it'll be toast and butter with our tea." She smiled at her husband and glanced over at the nearby table. It was full of various tools and devices and one particular pale blue vial containing an odd, glowing liquid.

"You've been making potions again, I see..." she observed while holding the blue vial aloft. The look on her face told Dr. Pipt he had been found out again.

"Yes dear," he confessed. The look on his face confirmed that he had, indeed, been found out.

The Emerald Slippers of Oz

"What kind of magic does this stuff do?" she asked while examining the blue glow within the vial.

"It's not magic, my dear," Dr. Pipt explained. "Just the right mix of berry juice and powdered cobalt and it glows for about a day or so. It's not even alchemy, I'm afraid...just chemistry."

"Do you wish to anger Princess Ozma or the Wizard of Oz?" Margolotte replied. She was quite concerned about angering the very people who had saved her life. "We have a good life here, even if it is a bit lonely."

"I know dear..." he said softly."I just can't help myself. The allure of the magic is very strong... even after so long."

For a moment or so, Dr. Pipt slid back into memory and recalled his days of old when he had magical powers... when he was very crooked and very skilled in the magical art of potions and powders.

He recalled fondly the years of stirring the four boiling pots of bronze, filled to the brim with the Powder of Life potion. There were six years of stirring in all and when he had finished, a scant handful of the bone white Powder of Life was all that remained.

   Its power to bring anything to Life was responsible
for bringing to Life the Glass Cat and Jack Pumpkinhead,
as well as the Sawhorse and the Gump. There was even an
unexpected animation of a phonograph named Victor
Columbia Edison when Dr. Pipt had used his latest batch
of the Powder of Life to bring to Life the Patchwork Girl,

whose name happened to be Scraps. A small amount had spilled onto the mechanical creation and soon, it was on its way through the Land of Oz, playing all manner of classical and jazz music.

By the time Dr. Pipt returned from his memory, Margolotte had returned with hot tea and milk, along with several well-buttered slices of toast.

"This will ease your mind," she assured her husband as she handed him a steaming hot cup and a slice of toast.

Before long, Dr. Pipt and Margolotte were seated by the far window, looking out at the mass of dark blue trees that surrounded the little blue house. The crackle of the fire in the fireplace soothed Dr. Pipt's nerves and Margolotte's calm, silent understanding helped the former crooked magician forget his craving for magic... at least for now.

Chapter 8
The Royal Emperor Of The Winkies

The following morning, after a sumptuous breakfast prepared by the Munchkin-turned-Winkie farmer's wife, Dorothy was once more on her way through the vast, yellow Winkie Country. On her waist was her trusty satchel, containing all manner of things a young Princess of Oz might need in a pinch.

She thought along the way about how the Tin Woodman was once himself a Munchkin, just like the farmer and his wife, with whom she had spent the night. The little girl from Kansas was glad she had not been around when Nick Chopper had been slowly transformed from a meat creature, as he had called himself, into his now-metal physique. Her musings and remembrances had made for a pleasant journey that passed the time quickly.

In less than an hour or so, the shining vision of the Tin Woodman's Tin Palace came into view.

Perched alongside the Winkie River, it made for a magnificent sight. The gleaming tin of the towers and parapets reflected the morning sun so that it clearly sparkled. Nearby, the river also reflected the gleaming sunlight as petite waves rippled across the pale blue surface.

Dorothy gasped, as she always did, when she would first catch sight of her good friend's place of residence. Its shining visage was overwhelming to all who encountered it, especially for the first time. This of course, was not Dorothy's first time... and yet once more, she gasped at its beauty.

She recalled well upon her return to Oz that the Tin Woodman had been made the Royal Emperor of the Winkies and how he had his palace of tin built along the smooth flowing waters of the Winkie River.

His rule as the Royal Emperor was both gentle and kind, with nary a disagreement among his subjects, the Winkies. Even when faced with difficult choices, his calm and pleasant demeanor persuaded all who came under his rule. The Land of the Winkies was a peaceful and quiet place.

Dorothy quickened her pace and before long, the bright shining tin gate, set within the dazzling tin walls that surrounded the Tin Palace, was standing tall before her.

As always, its gates were wide open and inviting to all who passed beneath them.

Once more, the dazzling beauty of the gleaming tin overwhelmed the little farm girl from Kansas. She took a moment to catch her breath, then made for the bright tin steps that lead up into the Grand Courtyard of the Tin Palace of the Royal Emperor of the Winkies. She was pleased to encounter once more, an old familiar sign at the base of the tin steps.

"Nick Chopper's place" read the engravings on the bright silver sign and Dorothy leapt up the steps and into the clear morning daylight of the Grand Courtyard.

"Dorothy!!!" shouted the Tin Woodman. He rattled and clanked a bit as he rushed forward to greet his dearest friend in all of Oz.

"Oh Tin Woodman!!!" Dorothy shouted back in reply. The two dear friends embraced for a moment, then went inside to visit and renew old acquaintances. Even though the two had seen each other only a few weeks before, Nick Chopper always reacted as though their separation had been years instead of days. It was, of course, because of his soft and tender heart, given to him by the Wizard of Oz, which overflowed with compassion and tenderness for everyone around him.

For the remainder of the day, Dorothy spoke of this and that... and even some of the other. She told the Tin Woodman about her plan to present Princess Ozma with a pair of Emerald Slippers.

"Promise you won't tell her!" Dorothy pleaded emphatically.

"Cross my heart!" replied Nick Chopper. He crossed his tin finger over the pocket that covered the place where the Wizard had cut into Him to insert his silken heart, stuffed with sawdust. Sticking out of the pocket was a fine, woven tin handkerchief, which Dorothy had suggested long ago.

"You still look so proper with that handkerchief," she added. "It's the perfect embellishment for a perfect gentleman!"

If the Tin Woodman could have blushed, he would

have turned a bright red, as though the tin surface had
been heated red-hot by an intense flame.

"Dorothy..." He gushed. For a moment, Nick
Chopper then thought about Dorothy's idea for a gift. She
had mentioned Ugu the Shoemaker, who was still a large
grey Dove, as far as she knew.

"I've seen a large nest in the highest tower of his
old Wicker Castle, which is to the west of here," he
explained. "I suspect he still lives there."

Dorothy paused to think about things.

"I've never had reason to judge him and he's never
caused any trouble since his enchantment," continued the
Tin Woodman. "I'm certain he'll agree to your request."

She thought some more, then nodded her head in
agreement with herself.

"Then I'll stay the night and head out in the
morning for the Wicker Castle of Ugu the Shoemaker!" she
declared.

Nick Chopper was, as always, thrilled to have his
dearest friend in all of Oz as his houseguest.

"Pardon me!" came a small, meek shout from below.
"I'm down here!"

The Royal Emperor of the Winkies stumbled a bit
as he side-stepped to avoid the nearby dragonfly who had
wandered into the gleaming confines of the Tin Palace.

"Whew!" He said, somewhat nervously. "I almost
hurt the poor thing." He and Dorothy watched as the
dragonfly flew off towards the large tin doors and out into
the Grand Courtyard.

Chapter 9
'Ol Mombi Dreams Up A Plan

Mombi woke up with a start from a dream in which she was being chased by the Scarecrow, the Tin Woodman, Glinda; Good Witch of the South and others. She had dropped her bag of magic potions all over the forest floor as she ran for her life. When she looked back, Mombi saw that it had all spilled out and had covered the mossy green surface of the ancient woods. She also noticed something very odd. There, gathering up all the potions and powders from the forest floor was Dr. Pipt.

Now, as she lay there, clutching her chest while her heart pounded, 'Ol Mombi tried to figure out why they were even chasing her to begin with.

Suddenly, a laugh burst out from her as she thought again of how much she wanted to be in control again and to practice magic once more.

Of course, there was still the notion that she had been stripped of her witchly powers and deprived of her ability to practice magic by Glinda.

"There has to be a way to regain my magical powers," Mombi thought to herself. *"And I will find a way!"*

Until the previous night, the old woman had never had a dream quite like this one. Now, 'Ol Mombi now knew what she needed to do. She had to prepare for a trip in search of Dr. Pipt and hopefully convince him to prepare another batch of his famous Powder of Life. Only then could she return to her old ways of magic and bring to Life her ancient powers.

That power was very intoxicating and even after all these years, she still desired to practice her witchly arts once more.

The old woman spent the morning making preparations for her journey and by mid-day, she was ready.

As she made her way out of her old home and on towards the nearby village, she passed by her only pig and her prized four-horned cow in the yard.

"You two take care until I return," she told them. Both animals grunted at the now-receding old woman, who was well on her way to find Dr. Pipt.

'Ol Mombi knew that the journey would be long and difficult for someone as old as her. She also knew that she would have to avoid Emerald City and Princess Ozma, who she regarded as her enemy, even though it had been Glinda; Good Witch of the South who had made the old witch drink a potion that stripped her of her magical powers.

"If I have to, I'll look up every witch, sorceress and magician I can find," Mombi thought to herself. "Then Dr. Pipt will have to grant my request. Only then will we once again practice our magic and be in control of all of Oz!"

The old woman cackled out loud at the thought of

regaining her powers and ruling over all of Oz.

"Then I'll teach that Ozma a lesson she'll never forget!" she shouted to no one but herself.

Chapter 10
The Wicker Castle

T
he following morning, the Tin Woodman
bid Dorothy a fond farewell and watched as
she headed westward towards the Wicker
Castle that was once home to Ugu the Shoemaker.

"Be careful, Dorothy," he warned his good friend.
"My heart tells me things aren't as they appear." The Tin
Woodman seemed uneasy about Dorothy's journey,
though he couldn't quite put his finger on why. He turned
and looked about for the buzzing sound he had heard only
moments before.

"There you are!" declared the Ruler of the Winkies.
He looked down at the green and black dragonfly that was
buzzing about the grounds of the Tin Palace. "I've got a
special request for you."

Dorothy found the journey westward to be both
pleasant and uneventful. Occasionally, she would stop to
rest and quench her thirst by a passing stream or nearby
spring, or grab a bite to eat from a local lunchpail tree.

By noontime, she had reached the valley that lead
down towards the high hill where the Wicker Castle of
Ugu the Shoemaker stood. In the distance, she could easily
see the silhouette of the Wicker Castle against the clear

blue skies of Oz.

    Dorothy quickened her pace and before long, the large wicker doors of Ugu the Shoemaker's former home stood proudly before her. As she looked around, Dorothy couldn't help but notice that she seemed to be the only person within the entire valley.

    "I hope he left them unlocked," she thought to herself. A sharp push against the brass railings that framed the doors and Dorothy was relieved to find that they opened quite easily.

    As she entered the main room of the castle, the

sound of the rushing winds passing through the open doors whistled softly and Dorothy stopped for a moment. Only the faint sound of the wind and the overwhelming silence of the Wicker Palace greeted her.

"Now how do I get to the high tower?" she asked out loud. There was no reply of course, and the Princess of Oz found herself quite alone in the castle.

Dorothy began exploring the various rooms and hallways until she found a spiral staircase that lead upwards into a grand tower of the finest wicker wood.

"Anyone home!" she shouted up through the ascending stairs. Dorothy waited for a reply and got only silence.

"Well," she said confidently, "The only way to go is up!"

Climbing the spiraling staircase, she made her way past several open doorways and a long hallway on the third floor. Dorothy remembered the words of her good friend, Nick Chopper and continued upwards towards the end of the spiral staircase.

As she climbed the staircase, she began to notice the presence of small twigs, which made a sharp snapping sound as she walked on them. More and more twigs, and even some straw began to litter the staircase as Dorothy climbed higher and higher. She could tell by a strong shaft of light piercing the room high above her that she was nearing the top of the tower.

"Hello?" she shouted up at the bright shaft of light. The stairs were now covered in twigs, small branches and a great deal of straw. There was still no answer as Dorothy continued her climb to the top of the tower.

Finally, Dorothy stepped gingerly onto the final step and looked about at the vast room which lay before her. The shaft of light now illuminated the room as it shone through the large window just above the large nest the nearly filled the room itself.

Dorothy gasped at the sight of the largest bird nest she had ever seen in her entire life.

Chapter 11
Blinkie Leaves Home

For several days, Blinkie paced frantically throughout her eight-sided house, thinking about her former glory as the leader of all the witches in Jinxland. She recalled with great delight all the magic she once performed and all the Evil she had brought down upon all the people in Jinxland.

In all the many years since she has been stripped of her magical prowess, Blinkie had never been able to regain her powers and her former glory as an Evil witch. In fact, she had never traveled out of sight of her old house since returning from the Quadling Country of Oz, powerless and alone. Now, she couldn't stop thinking about regaining her magic and the thought of traveling abroad filled her with delight.

Blinkie considered finding all of the old witches of Jinxland and convincing them to join in her cause to regain her powers, but the ugly old woman with the black eye patch knew that getting all the witches to agree to her plans was futile. She had been a cruel, Evil leader who was both hated and feared.

"No one's gonna help this old woman," she thought to herself while looking out over the vast forest that ran along the border of Jinxland. *"Not after how Evil I was."* She cackled loudly at the thought of her former Evilness.

"I can't count on my old friend, the Wicked Witch of the South," she muttered out loud, remembering how

The Emerald Slippers of Oz

Glinda had defeated the old hag long ago and taken over as the Ruler of the Quadling Country, south of the Emerald Countryside, where the Emerald City resided.

She knew that another of her old witch friends, the Wicked Witch of the East had been destroyed by a little girl long ago. There was also a rumor that her friend's sister, the Wicked Witch of the West had also fallen victim to the same little girl, though Blinkie didn't believe in rumors.

"Surely there must be a witch or two that still lives," she thought hopefully. Blinkie thought long and hard about her plans for regaining her magic.

While searching about the grounds of her home for some mushrooms and roots, Blinkie had another thought and recalled a long forgotten memory.

"What about Mombi?" she said out loud, frightening the few birds who were perched in the nearby trees. "Surely Mombi still lives?!"

The ugly old woman remembered the old sorceress who lived in the far northern Gillikin Country of Oz. The two had been friends at one time, or at least as close to friends as two ugly old witches could ever be.

Now, the thought of finding Mombi consumed the former leader of the Jinxland witches and filled her thoughts with Evil delight.

"She'll know how to help me find my magic!" exclaimed Blinkie. The excitement of it all was more than the old woman could handle and she settled down for the night, dreaming of Evil magic spells and potions and other such things.

The next morning, Blinkie made preparations for the long journey and gathered together a few essentials she felt she might need. In her black bag were the mushrooms and roots she had gathered the day before, along with a water gourd and some cheese.

"Where did I put that Pepperspice box?" the old woman muttered out loud. She didn't want to leave it behind in case she found herself facing a bland soup or stew along the way.

After a few minutes of searching, the old woman found it right where she had left it the other day.

"There you are!" she declared, grabbing the old Pepperspice box and stuffing into her trusty black bag. "Now we can be on our way!"

Blinkie headed out the door, grabbing an old walking stick that was leaning up against the outside doorframe. She headed north towards the dark, foreboding forest that spread out before her in the distance. Where it began, Blinkie knew that was the border between Jinxland and the Quadling Country of Oz. She hadn't ventured very far into that old forest since her days as the leader of the Jinxland witches. Now Blinkie was on a journey that would take her as far into Oz as she had ever been before.

For hours, the old woman with the black eye patch walked slowly and deliberately through the dark forest, always keeping to the very narrow trail that led northward, eventually spilling out into Munchkin

The Emerald Slippers of Oz

Country. The journey was hard on the old woman's body and she stopped every now and then to rest and quench her thirst.

She would continue on after every stop, walking slowly through the damp, dark forest until fatigue compelled her to stop once more for rest and some water... or a bite of cheese.

The forest was so thick that, after a time, the narrow trail was nearly impossible to follow and it made walking very difficult at best. This didn't bother Blinkie thought too much because it gave her time to think... and ponder all the possibilities that regaining her magic would bring.

Along the way, she studied each flower, each plant, each leaf and wondered if perhaps these might help her regain her magic. The deeper she went into the forest, the more exotic the fauna and flora became. She renewed her tempo and her mood grew darker with each step.

Blinkie wondered how far along she had traveled through the dark forest. It was clear that no one had traveled the nearly invisible path in ages. Only a witch would even consider it, given how dark and foreboding the surrounding forest truly seemed.

She came across an old log that had fallen long ago and the old woman sat down to rest once more. Her bones now ached from the arduous journey and Blinkie sat there, somewhat breathless, yet aware of the roots and moss that surrounded the old log.

She looked through her old black bag and studied

the mushrooms and other roots, leaves and lichen she had gathered earlier that morning. Somewhere in her now deranged mind, she knew that if she looked hard enough, she was certain that she would find the very things she desperately needed for her magic.

"*Oh well,*" she thought to herself. "*This forest can't go one forever.*"

The old woman got up and stretched out her arms, trying to push out the dull ache that throbbed within them. She started walking once more northward, as best she could tell. The trail was no more and Blinkie had to step over fallen limbs and small bushes to make her way forward. She stopped a moment and strained to hear something in the distance. All that morning, the damp, dark forest had been strangely silent, unprepared for the invasion of an old woman whose Evil deeds and intentions were just now returning to the surface.

Now, a gurgling sound appeared from somewhere nearby, and Blinkie continued on, the walking stick now more in use than ever before. As she struggled through the thick undergrowth, the gurgling sound grew louder and Blinkie recognized the sounds of running water.

Sweat ran down her forehead as Blinkie wiped it away from her black eye patch. Her thoughts wandered back to the day the Scarecrow had defeated her and removed her power.

"One of these days, I'll meet up with him again," she mused, "and we'll see just how strong his powers really are!"

"Yes..." she continued musing, "I'll show him who's more powerful..."

Before long, the forest thinned out just a bit and

gave way to a clearing where a small spring sprang forth from the forest floor and became a clear blue stream. The path of the small stream led onwards towards an ever-growing light that Blinkie knew signaled the end of the dark forest and her journey through the woods.

Blinkie stopped by the spring and refilled her water gourd. She then finished the last of the cheese which she had packed that morning and felt great relief. She could tell that the sun was nearing the far eastern horizon to her left as the shadows from the trees grew long in the clearing.

The old woman decided to make camp for the night and before long, sleep had overtaken her and returned her to dreams of magic, glory and Evil.

Chapter 12
The Journey of 'Ol Mombi

By late afternoon, 'Ol Mombi was soaked in sweat from the exertion of the journey and the brisk pace she had tried to maintain. The thought of finding Dr. Pipt and how she might convince him to help her had driven her onward, but she was not used to such a hard walk, for it had been a long time since she had done so.

The old woman had been traveling southward for most of the morning and had decided to sit down on an old log that had fallen near a stream long ago. She sipped on some sassafras tea from her water gourd that she had brewed that morning. Her thoughts wandered here and there as she looked about the vast yellow countryside of Winkie Country.

She thought about the old stone castle of the Wicked Witch of the East, which she had passed by earlier that morning. Though it was now an empty shell of its former Evil following the demise of its former occupant, the dark, foreboding stone seemed to almost call out to her and invite her in.

"When I get my powers back, I'll make that place my new home..." she said out loud.

For now, 'Ol Mombi was more concerned with the journey ahead of her.

In the far distance, she could see the sunlight glinting off the shiny tin surface of the Castle of the Tin Woodman.

"I best be heading east soon and avoid that infernal man of tin!" she thought to herself. 'Ol Mombi recalled that the Tin Woodman was a good friend of both Glinda and Princess Ozma and she feared being discovered before her journey had hardly begun.

After a few more sips of tea and a few bites from a small biscuit she had retrieved from her satchel, 'Ol Mombi got up and resumed walking, though now she decided on a more leisurely pace.

The smooth cobblestone road that headed south came across another smooth cobblestone road which headed east towards Emerald City. The old woman turned to the east and quickened her pace just a bit.

To the south of her, the old woman could just barely see the top of the Scarecrow's Tower, which resembled a gigantic ear of corn and served as his home.

She spied a lone crow flying towards her and 'Ol Mombi ducked under the cover of a nearby tree so as not to be seen by the flying bird of black.

'Ol Mombi recalled that the local crows served the Scarecrow as both messengers and servants and she feared she might yet be discovered.

After a few minutes, the skies were clear of any birds and the old woman continued on her way eastward. She felt much better at the thought of leaving the yellow countryside of the Winkies behind her.

Having spent most of her life in the Gillikin Country, which is predominantly purple in color, the old woman and former sorceress found the color yellow far too bright for her liking. It reminded her of the brightness of the sunlight and she had always preferred the darkness of purple, which reminded her more of deep twilight and the nighttime.

Within an hour of turning east, the countryside had gone from mostly yellow to almost entirely green and 'Ol Mombi knew she was now in the lands that surrounded the Emerald City. Every now and then, she would pass by others walking on the road, most of whom would wave at her and greet her warmly. 'Ol Mombi chose not to speak to any of them and generally kept to herself.

The sun began making its way towards the far eastern horizon as 'Ol Mombi continued her journey eastward, alone in her thoughts. Her shadow grew longer as she pondered a memory of the old Poppy Fields that ran along the Munchkin River. The old woman remembered a story she once heard about how Dorothy and the Cowardly Lion had been lulled to sleep by the deadly fumes of the beautiful red flowers, only to be rescued by the Queen of the Field Mice and Her subjects. They had helped the Scarecrow and the Tin Woodman pull the Cowardly Lion out of the Poppy Fields on a large wooden wagon the Tin Woodman had built.

"What a shame those lousy little rodents had come along," she thought to herself. *"When I get my powers back, I'll destroy every one of those filthy little vermin!"* 'Ol Mombi did not like mice at all, nor any other small creatures that scurried about.

Just then, an idea began forming in the old woman's mind that seemed very pleasant to her. She thought about the deadly power of the Poppies and how she might use them to her advantage. As the former sorceress contemplated her plan, she looked up to see that the sun was nearly upon the far eastern horizon. Nightfall would be upon her soon and 'Ol Mombi decided to settle down for the night.

Although Lake Quad was just to the south of her, dotted along the shoreline with houses and docks and all manner of sailing vessels, once again, 'Ol Mombi decided to keep to herself and lay low.

Fortunately, a Lunchpail Tree stood nearby with many low hanging branches and the old woman decided this would be a good place to bed down for the night.

After a hardy meal from the tree, 'Ol Mombi felt very tired and settled up against the trunk of tree and looked northward at the faint green glow that was Emerald City. Although the glow made her somewhat nervous, she knew she was far enough away so as not to be discovered by Princess Ozma.

Before long, the old woman had drifted off to sleep

The Emerald Slippers of Oz

with dreams of conquest and magic dancing in her head.

Chapter 13
Dorothy's Request Of Ugu The Grey Dove

I t took Dorothy a few minutes to gather her thoughts after reaching the top of the tower where Ugu's nest now resided. The immense size of it had completely caught her off guard and Dorothy thought back to her last encounter with Ugu the Shoemaker.

Following his transformation into a dove, Ugu had been offered the opportunity to be transformed back into a person by Dorothy, who had forgiven his transgressions and recognized his repentance.

Ugu however, knew that the ways of magic would corrupt him once more and he had requested to remain a dove so that he may retain his peaceful and loving ways. It had been many long years since that transformation and Dorothy wondered if Ugu the Shoemaker might be persuaded to return to the life of a person and resume his shoemaking ways. She was certain she could convince him that, after his many years as a dove that he might yearn to return to his old ways, hopeful now that he no longer

68

The Emerald Slippers of Oz

desired the ways of magic.

"Hello!" shouted the little farm girl from Kansas. The echoed reply confirmed that no one was home. The large room at the top of the grand tower of the Wicker Castle was nearly filled by the huge nest and Dorothy wondered what his life had been like for all these years.

"Now what do I do?" she pondered out loud. Having found Ugu's nest, she had thought it would be a matter of simply asking him to return to his old cobbler's trade in order to make her a pair of Emerald Slippers for Princess Ozma. She hadn't counted on him not being at home.

Dorothy sat down on a nearby step and decided to wait a while in hopes that Ugu might return home. In her satchel was a loaf of honey-wheat bread and peaches which the Munchkin-turned-Winkie farmer's wife had prepared for her journey. She was glad to have it now and ate her fill, quenching her thirst along the way from the water jug she always carried with her on her journeys across Oz.

For more than an hour, she waited patiently for Ugu and thought about how she might convince him to fulfill her request for the Emerald Slippers. During that time, she looked about the giant nest and marveled at the intricate craftsmanship that Ugu had displayed in building his home. It seemed to her that the nest might accommodate several birds at once and she wondered if perhaps Ugu now had a family of his own.

Just then, a fluttering of wings sounded through

the open window and moments later, a rather plain-looking gray dove flew in and alighted gently upon the edge of the giant nest.

It was, of course, Ugu the Grey Dove and he instantly recognized the little farm girl from Kansas who had defeated him so long ago and transformed into the gray dove he was now.

"Dorothy!" he said rather excitedly. "Why, I can't believe it's you!"

Dorothy smiled and approached the grey dove. "It's wonderful to see you again, Ugu," she replied.

Ugu hoped down from the edge of the nest and fluttered his wings just a bit.

"In all these years, you are the first and only human visitor I've ever had here in my lonely home," Ugu said

70

sadly. "Why have you come to visit me?"

"I wanted to see how you were doing and perhaps offer you a chance to return to your former self," she explained. "It's been many years and I thought that maybe you might like to become a shoemaker once more."

The grey dove paced around a bit, preening his feathers and cooing a bit as he pondered Dorothy's reason for visiting. The two talked of this and that... and even some of the other. She asked him about the immense nest he had built and Ugu confessed that he had thought to start a family of his own, but no other doves would have him since they knew that he was, in fact, only a grey dove by transformation and not by birth.

Dorothy could see that this caused Ugu some grief and she quickly changed the subject. They spoke of witches and the Wizard, who was now the Royal Magician in service to Princess Ozma.

"Is she doing well," he asked Dorothy. "I mean, after being a peach pit and all, I thought she might still be angry with me?"

The Emerald Slippers of Oz

Dorothy laughed gently at Ugu's concern.

"Of course not, you silly bird!" she declared. "Princess Ozma is even more forgiving than I am!"

At the mention of Princess Ozma's name, Ugu the Grey Dove could sense that Dorothy had something else on her mind... and it somehow involved Princess Ozma.

"Is that the only reason you came to visit me in my Wicker Castle nest. I think you have something else in mind in asking me to return to my former trade as a shoemaker," he said slyly.

Dorothy blushed a bit, knowing that the grey dove had sensed her thoughts and plans. She spoke of her desire to present her dearest friend, Princess Ozma with a pair of Emerald Slippers for her birthday later in the year.

"I want so much to give her a gift truly worthy of a princess and everyone I've spoken to agrees that you were the only one who could produce such a wonderful pair of royal slippers," Dorothy explained. "Please, won't you grant my request and return to your cobbler's trade?"

Ugu the Grey Dove preened himself some more and paced about at a more frantic pace than before. He excused himself and flew out the window in order to think the matter over.

"I think better when I'm flying," he had explained.

Dorothy sat back down on the nearby step and awaited Ugu's return and his decision.

Ugu flew about the grand tower for several minutes, then headed off to the south-east and the nearby village of Herku, where he once owned a small cobbler's shop and from where he had begun his life of magic long ago. When he reached the small village, he was pleased to see that old shop still remained. The grey dove flew down and landed on a nearby branch near his old shop and looked around at the remains of his former life.

Within, the tools of the cobbler's trade had been left in their place as though he had only been gone a few days or so. Still in place were the leather cutters and shoe stands where he affixed the soles with hammer and tacks. On the walls were the instruments of the cobbler's trade, hanging on their proper hooks and awaiting their master's return. Ugu the Grey Dove was pleased that his old place had been left to remain as he had left it so long ago.

73

The Emerald Slippers of Oz

Suddenly, a lone figure entered from the back room and wandered about the shop, looking over the tools of the trade and admiring the various instruments of the cobbler's wares.

He was young man, by most standards, bearing a head of short, golden blonde hair and a muscular frame that spoke of his youthful exuberance. One of the most noticeable things about his appearance was the lack of shoes upon his feet.

Ugu the Grey Dove flew away in confusion and made quickly for the Wicker Castle and his nest.

Chapter 14
'Ol Mombi And The
Field Of Poppies

The morning sun greeted 'Ol Mombi with brilliant rays and the songs of nearby birds, playing in the Lunchpail Tree. All around was sunshine and the ever-present green glow to the north.

Even at high noon, the green glow from Emerald City would be easily visible to anyone within the Emerald countryside that surrounded the capital of Oz.

Now, 'Ol Mombi could see it too, and it was early in the morning. The old woman stretched and moaned, her morning routine not so routine anymore since she began her journey to find Dr. Pipt. She had slept well, but dreams of past glories and her defeat at the hands of Glinda: Good Witch of the South ran circles through her mind as she prepared for the day's journey.

Within the hour, 'Ol Mombi was on her way along the cobblestone path that ran along the southern countryside which surrounded Emerald City. She made good time as she walked slowly but confidently along the green stones that passed perilously close to the ancient home of Princess Ozma... and discovery. The old woman felt certain her presence would not be noticed among the numerous others traveling through Oz.

As 'Ol Mombi continued eastward and south of Emerald City, she was deep in thought as she pondered the deadly Poppy Fields that ran along the Munchkin River.

"If they put people to sleep," she thought to herself, *"then perhaps they can be used to my advantage."* She knew this path lead north once it entered Munchkin Country, but recalled a small goat path that lead directly south to the Field of Poppies and their deadly fragrance.

The old woman cackled softly as she was passed by several country folk, dressed in blue and looking puzzled at the laughing old woman. She decided that she would collect some of the spicy, pungent flowers of scarlet known as Poppies and keep them safe in her black bag.

"The only thing is the odor..." 'Ol Mombi mused out loud. She went back to her innermost thoughts as she made her way east.

Before long, a memory from long ago found its way back into 'Ol Mombi's thoughts and she recalled having picked the Poppies before.

Once again, a soft cackle emerged from the old woman.

Just then, she noticed that the countryside was now a pronounced blue color, both in flora and fauna. The local houses, fence rows, and even the field grass was a varied array of blues, both light and dark.

The old woman felt a sense of relief at having escaped the notice of Princess Ozma and she quickened her step. She had only been traveling for a couple of hours by now and 'Ol Mombi entertained numerous thoughts about magical spells, transformations and her return to power as a sorceress.

By noontime, 'Ol Mombi came to a sharp bend in the now-blue cobblestone path that ran through Munchkin Country. The path continued northward while 'Ol Mombi looked southward, searching for the old, barely seen goat path that led to the Field of Poppies just over the far horizon.

It didn't take long for someone who actually wanted to find the path, though to the uninterested eye, it appeared nearly invisible.

There, between a small cleft in the blue hedgerow that ran along the hill was the small goat path leading south over the far hill.

'Ol Mombi turned southward and stepped through the small cleft, heading along the nearly unnoticeable path towards a faint hint of a pungent, spicy smell.

After an hour of slow progress, 'Ol Mombi caught sight of the bright patch of scarlet red flowers just ahead in the near distance. She came to a small creek and sat down on a fallen log that had washed up on shore. Since she had not eaten anything all morning, the old woman retrieved an old metal cup from her black bag and quenched her thirst while enjoying some homemade bread and honey.

The Emerald Slippers of Oz

After a much deserved rest alongside the small creek, 'Ol Mombi coaxed herself into getting up. The faint odor of Poppies was all around and the old woman feared she would not wake up if she didn't get up now.

'Ol Mombi pulled out an old scarf that she carried in her pocket and dipped it into the slowly flowing blue waters of the small creek. She tied the scarf around her face, being certain to cover both her mouth and nose, as she now remembered doing long ago. She had discovered that doing this protected her from the effects of the Poppies' fragrance. The memory of picking Poppy Flowers was now strong in her mind as she made her way into the scarlet red flowers that ran south as far as the Munchkin River. 'Ol Mombi found she could walk through the Poppy Fields without falling asleep and this made her journey a little bit easier.

The former sorceress now set herself upon the task of picking just the right flowers for an idea that was just starting to brew in her mind. She picked and discarded numerous flowers, keeping only the perfect ones she felt would *"do the job."*

After half an hour or so, 'Ol Mombi looked up to see a passing boat that was occupied by a lone sailor, poling the boat as quickly as he could past the deadly fumes. He too had a wet rag covering his mouth and nose, as did his passenger, who was an old woman, as best as 'Ol Mombi could tell.

'Ol Mombi stared hard at the passenger, who appeared to have a black eye patch over her left eye. The old woman on the boat stared equally hard back at 'Ol Mombi.

She thought long and hard about the old woman on the boat as the raft vanished around the bend, heading westward towards Lake Quad.

Something familiar about the old woman haunted 'Ol Mombi as she headed out of the Field of Poppies and headed east for the Great Lower Fork of the Munchkin River.

Chapter 15
Ugu the Shoemaker

Dorothy wandered about the empty Wicker Castle and marveled at how well it had been built. She recalled her adventures with Ugu the Shoemaker.

She thought back to long ago when she had sought Ugu the Shoemaker-turned Evil magician with her friends, Toto, the Cowardly Lion, the Wizard of Oz, Scraps the Patchwork Girl, the Sawhorse, and others.

The Wicker Castle had many twists and turns that Ugu had built within to confuse those who would try to capture him. There was also a mighty cage down below that Ugu would lock himself away in to protect himself from his enemies.

Dorothy chuckled as she recalled how the wicker rooms could be turned upside-down to send his enemies falling head-over-teakettles while he remained upright and safe.

"I'm certainly glad the old place has settled down," she thought to herself.

The Emerald Slippers of Oz

Suddenly, Dorothy heard the gentle flap of wings resonating from the Grand Tower and Ugu's nest. She made her way quickly up the winding, spiral staircase and came upon a very agitated bird.

Ugu the Grey Dove was prancing back and forth so rapidly as to be only a blur of his former self, or so Dorothy thought as she watched while trying to catch her breath. He was quite distraught at the thought of someone living in his former home. Ugu had flown by the old place only a few days before and no one appeared to be living there.

Now, someone was home... and it wasn't Ugu.

"What is wrong, Ugu?" Dorothy asked the grey dove, once both of them had calmed down a bit. She gathered that something was not right with Ugu and thought how she might help her former foe.

Ugu was in no mood to talk, but he also knew that it was Dorothy who had defeated him long ago and transformed him into the dove he now was. He paced and hopped a bit, then settled onto the edge of his nest to gather his thoughts.

"There is someone living in my old shop back in Herku," Ugu said in a somewhat fearful tone. "A young man, blonde of hair and... wearing no shoes."

Dorothy understood immediately why Ugu was upset. She thought back to her arrival and first few years in Oz. Often she would return to Munchkin City to "check up on the place," she would say nearly every time. The visits to her old farm house soon grew less and less as the years passed by. In time, Dorothy had settled into life in Oz quite well, as her Aunt Em and Uncle Henry. She no longer dwelled on Kansas, thinking of Oz now as her home.

One day, after an absence of over a year, Dorothy visited Munchkin City and found something amiss with her old house. The thought of someone living in it hadn't occurred to her and the little farm girl from Kansas found herself suddenly frightened, though only a little.

Dorothy soon discovered that the Munchkins had only put up a golden picket fence, which stood nearly as tall as the tallest Munchkin in town. They had also begun transforming the yard surrounding the old ramshackle house into a beautiful garden of flowers, bearing countless varieties of roses, daffodils and sunflowers. To one side of the house, the Munchkins had nearly completed construction of what the lead Munchkin in charge of construction called "a marble hall, dedicated to Dorothy, who set us free from the Wicked Witch of the East!" The rest of the crew cheered loudly, happy at their work.

Dorothy was both pleased and somewhat embarrassed by all the attention. The little farm girl from Kansas blushed often during that visit, especially when the Munchkins unveiled their bust of Dorothy, carved from the purest white marble, which had come from the far side of Mount Munch, by the Shifting Sands.

Now, Ugu the Grey Dove was faced with a similar problem and Dorothy knew she had come at the right time, and at the right place.

Dorothy could see that Ugu had regained his senses and had calmed down a great deal. After a bit of silence, with only the whistling of the winds within earshot, Dorothy approached the subject of her visit once more.

"Would you please return to being a person, and shoemaker, and grant my request to make Princess Ozma the loveliest Emerald Slippers you possibly can?" Dorothy pleaded with Ugu. She was even more certain now that Ugu desired a return to the life of his youth, and the art of shoemaking.

Ugu considered Dorothy's plea for a full minute while the winds continued their song. He knew from her first appearance by his nest that he might return to his old ways... though there was a few of which he did not want to repeat.

"Yes, Dorothy. I'll grant your request and you may free me of this avian body and return me to my former self," he spoke clearly and with great conviction. Ugu felt suddenly giddy at the thought of making shoes once more. The thought of magic had yet to surface and Ugu would not allow it anyway. He was certain he could regain his life as a cobbler. The cutting of leather and sewing of sinew and thread would be his once more and the gray dove cooed loudly with delight.

Dorothy felt giddy too, certain that all would be well and *"Princess Ozma will soon have her new Emerald Slippers,"* she thought to herself.

She reached into her satchel, which hung neatly by her side, and retrieved the Magic Belt from within. One quick swing around her waist and the Magic Belt promptly snapped into place, fitting the little farm girl quite snuggly.

Dorothy had, of course, borrowed the Magic Belt from the Toy Room of the Wizard of Oz, where Princess Ozma had chosen to keep it. The Princess and Ruler of Oz often wandered about her Royal Palace in Emerald City, and the Wizard of Oz's Toy Room presented lots of wonderful, magical toys to marvel over, especially since Princess Ozma required no apparatus nor devices of legerdemain to conjure Her magic. The one device that served Her royal needs was the Magic Picture, which upon demand could show the viewer anyplace in Oz... and on a rare occasion, the Great Outside.

Dorothy had chosen to use the power of the Magic Belt to return Ugu to human form since it had been the Magic Belt that had transformed him in the first place. Being a princess herself and permitted by Royal Decree to practice magic, Dorothy thought nothing of using the magical device.

Now, Ugu was standing before her, nearly ready to become human once more when a thought crossed his mind.

"What if the desire of magic should return?" he thought to himself as Dorothy inhaled a breath and spoke the wish for the Magic Belt to hear.

"I wish that Ugu the Shoemaker be restored to his former self and return to his life of cobblery," she spoke clearly and with great certainty. The little farm girl from Kansas then turned to Ugu the Grey Dove and watched with great anticipation.

The Emerald Slippers of Oz

Ugu felt the transformation begin almost immediately and shuddered one last time as a bird might do. The slick, smooth feathers that had made up his plumage soon took on the shape of a shirt, while his breast feathers, being downier that the rest, took on the appearance of trousers.

Meanwhile, inside the transforming apparel, Ugu quickly returned to the form of a man, old and somewhat bent, though only a little. His face bore a look of bewilderment as bird became man and Ugu returned to his former self. His shirt was of rough linen, brown in color and upon his head was a long grey feather protruding from an old leather cap that had seen better days.

In a moment's time, Ugu regained his senses and looked down upon his body. His arms outstretched, Ugu giggled with delight at the old sensations returning to his mind. He walked about and flapped his arms, as if to remind himself he was no longer a bird.

All the while, Dorothy watched as the Magic Belt worked its magic and transformed Ugu back into a shoemaker. She delighted in his glee at being restored to his former self.

There was much celebration until Ugu suddenly recalled his flight home and why he had flown back in such haste.

"There's someone living in my old shop!" he cried out as he fell to the floor, somewhat exhausted by the whole transformational process.

The Emerald Slippers of Oz

Dorothy sat with Ugu the Shoemaker and told him everything that had happened in Oz since their last meeting... or as much as she knew. She spoke of Mombi, who Ugu remembered as "being most foul a witch as any eastern or western witch I ever heard of!"

They spoke of Emerald Slippers and Ozma's birthday, of lions and tigers and bears...

"Oh my!" Ugu shouted with a fearful tone, recalled from his days as a bird, trying to avoid being the prey of a lion, tiger or bear.

By the time Dorothy had finished, it was nearly sunset and Dorothy wished for "supper and pleasant night's rest."

Ugu decided to wander the surrounding lands during the night and consider his thoughts, many of which were consumed by the stranger in his old shop back in Herku. His strength had returned following the sumptuous meal Dorothy had provided and Ugu was in no mood for sleep. Besides, as a bird, he had always been in his nest by sundown and up at sunrise. Now he could enjoy the night in all its splendor.

"See you in the morning, Dorothy," Ugu said politely as he bid Dorothy goodnight and headed out to explore the valley surrounding the Wicker Castle.

Chapter 16
Blinkie And 'Ol Mombi's Near Miss

Blinkie woke up, refreshed and ready to start another long day. She ate a quick breakfast and looked out across the small stream that gushed forth from the nearby spring, thinking about the journey ahead of her.

"Oh well..." she thought, *"I best get up and start moving. Them witches ain't gonna find themselves..."*

Now, the forest wasn't so dark and foreboding and Blinkie could see more daylight than darkness.

"Just like myself, this forest was dark and foreboding, as are all witches..." she continued musing to herself.*"Well, most witches. And hopefully I'll find a witch who'll help me with my magic."*

Blinkie still couldn't find a trail, but it didn't matter now that she had found the spring. She knew that she would soon find her way out of the woods.

The morning slowly wore on as she walked and rested, following the stream towards the ever-increasing light.

The Emerald Slippers of Oz

Finally, she had reached the last of the woods and stepped out into a clearing. Behind her was the dark forest and before her was the Munchkin River, which she could clearly see flowing northward towards the far horizon.

After a light brunch of pears from a nearby orchard that ran along the river, Blinkie followed the flowing blue waters until she came upon a very small village by a fork in the river.

The village was a typical village by Munchkin standards, supplying various fruits and vegetables from the nearby orchards and farmlands and shipping them downstream along the Munchkin River.

Blinkie soon came upon a small boat with an old man bent over it, loading supplies onto the deck. She thought about how hard her journey had been so far and how much easier it might be to ride the river.

"Could you make room for an old lady in your boat, kind sir?" she asked him politely.

The old man looked up from his task.

"I don't see a lady," he thought to himself. He smiled and kept his thought to himself.

"Where be you headin'?" he asked Blinkie politely.

Blinkie thought for a moment, unwilling to reveal her true reasons for her journey across Oz.

"I just wanna see some countryside, if you don't mind me tagging along?" she explained. "I can pay my way if you could find a spot for me."

"I'll make some stops at other villages to trade and barter for supplies and such for my own village... but yea,

you can ride along. The only payment I need is some polite
conversation, if you don't mind?" he replied. The old man
was actually pleased to have some company on his
journey, since he normally made his trips downriver alone.

Blinkie agreed and watched as the old man loaded
the last of his supplies, then she boarded the boat and the
two slowly made their way along the river.

"This is so much better than walking any day," she
thought to herself as the blue landscape of Munchkin
Country floated slowly by. *"Much better..."*

Each village was a little different than the one
before and Blinkie kept an eye out for various plants, roots,
flowers and herbs that she thought might come in handy.
She occasionally picked some of interest and put them in
her black bag.

At one village, Blinkie had to purchase another bag
just to accommodate the amount of herbs and flowers she
had picked along the way.

The old man had noticed her odd ways and
wondered why the old woman needed such odd plants
and roots.

"Why all the flower pickin' and such?" he asked her
purchase of the extra bag.

Blinkie felt a moment of panic, thinking that the old
man had guessed her plans. She breathed deeply, then
thought up a quick lie.

"These are for a special tea that helps me with my
old bones," she said with some hesitation.

The old man thought nothing more of her

explanation and continued on with his conversation. In between villages, as the blue waters flowed slowly past the bow of the small boat, Blinkie and the old man spoke of many things. There were rumors of gnomes and dragons, as well as Princess Ozma's latest birthday.

Blinkie had asked casually about some of the old witches from long ago and the old man was more than happy to talk on and on about how each had been either destroyed or rendered powerless.

"Seems like every witch or wizard has gone away," the old man suggested. "Ain't heard hide 'nor hair 'bout any of 'em for the longest time."

Blinkie said little during the old man's history lesson, but she was sadly disappointed that there were no witches or wizards about anymore.

"There has to be someone left who remembers the old ways of magic?" she thought to herself.

Late in the day, Blinkie could see a bright red field of flowers off in the distance to the north of the river. She watched as the old man dipped several pieces of blue cloth in the water and held out one to her.

"You'll need to cover your nose and mouth, 'lest you fall asleep," he said. "We be coming upon the Poppy Fields."

"Oh thank you, thank you!" she exclaimed as she tied the wet blue cloth around her face. She recalled how deadly the Poppy Fields were and was grateful the old man had known what to do.

The old man reached down for a long pole and

began poling the boat faster downstream, hoping to lessen the time they would be in amongst the deadly fumes.

Before long, the bright red poppies were directly beside the small boat. The field of flowers went on for as far as the old man and Blinkie could see.

Blinkie looked across the bright red flowers and saw a strange old woman, bent over and picking poppies.

"Why in Oz would she pick those?" she thought to herself. *"Unless she was a witch... No, she couldn't be another witch, could she?"*

The old man was too consumed with poling the boat as fast as he could past the Poppy Fields to even notice the old woman among the scarlet flowers.

Blinkie continued staring at the old woman, wondering to herself about the odd appearance among the Poppies.

Just then, the old woman in the Poppy Field stood up and looked directly at Blinkie.

"She does look kinda familiar...." Blinkie wondered to herself. She noticed that the old woman among the Poppies also had a cloth tied around her face so that only her eyes were visible.

Blinkie watched the old woman while the small boat slowly made its way past the immense field of scarlet flowers. As the small boat slowly rounded the bend in the river and out of sight of the Poppy Fields, Blinkie could see that the old woman in the flowers was still staring at her.

Chapter 17
Pacifico; The Cobbler's Apprentice

T he following morning saw the Great Sun of Oz rise as Ugu returned from his nightlong journey through the local countryside. It had been many years since he had walked on his own two human legs and the experience had filled Ugu with great joy.

He marveled at the vast valley where his Wicker Palace was located, taking in all the nighttime sights and sounds that he could never enjoy when he was a grey dove, nor when he was consumed with the pursuit of magic and power over all of Oz.

Ugu was especially pleased at the night sky, resplendent in all its glory. The moon, nearly full, had illuminated the landscape in an eerie, ethereal glow that transformed the trees into ghostly specters and the flowing Winkie River to the west into a silvery path leading off into the far darkness of the Ozian countryside.

The stunning beauty of the night had even taken Ugu's mind off of the startling discovery he had made at his old shop back in Herku. Now, with the return of daylight, came the realization that his old shop was now occupied by a stranger.

Dorothy found Ugu sitting on the edge of his old birds nest, fretting about the stranger in his shop and muttering to himself.

"What do you wanna do about the stranger in your shop?" Dorothy asked Ugu.

Ugu shook his head, unsure of what he should do next.

Dorothy knew that if Ugu was going to make a fine pair of Emerald Slippers, he was going to have to reclaim his old shop… and his old life as a cobbler.

They headed down the spiral staircase and soon found themselves on the road leading through the valley and eastward towards the old village of Herku.

Before long, Dorothy and Ugu had stopped by a small stream for a rest and a bite to eat from a familiar lunchpail tree.

Perched next to the lunchpail tree was her old friend from Kansas, Billina the Hen.

"How nice to see you, Billina!" she exclaimed.

"What brings you around this part of Oz?"

Billina clucked and pecked at the ground.

"I'm headed back home to Emerald City after visiting some of my chicks who now live up in the country of the Yips," the old hen replied.

Dorothy laughed and reached up to grab a couple of ripe lunch pails. She handed one to Ugu, who took it gratefully.

"Well, I'll be heading off now, Dorothy. I'm certain my younger chicks must be missing me by now," the old hen clucked.

Dorothy smiled and watched as Billina made her way along the road and was soon out of sight.

Dorothy now turned her attention to Ugu and watched as he opened his very ripe lunchpail. A broad smile crossed his face and Dorothy laughed.

"Why are you so happy, Ugu?" she asked.

"Peanut butter sandwiches!!!" he cried out. "I haven't had one of these in so long!"

The two sat and ate and laughed by the side of the small stream.

She spoke of how her and Billina had arrived in Oz long ago by means of an old chicken coop, caught up in a vicious storm while Dorothy was traveling across the ocean to Australia with her Uncle Henry.

Ugu laughed as she described the immense gale that had brought her to Oz.

Dorothy was pleased that Ugu was regaining his sense of person, his inner self returning to the surface of who he was. She was convinced that a happy Ugu could easily produce a beautiful pair of Emerald Slippers. She was also happy that Ugu seemed to be free of any bad thoughts about magic and his former life as a grey dove.

After a time, Ugu and Dorothy returned to the cobblestone road that led eastward towards Herku.

By noontime, the village of Herku was visible in the distance.

Ugu recognized the four square walls that surrounded the old town, as did Dorothy.

Ugu grew somewhat apprehensive at the site of the burnished copper gate that served as the only entrance into the city. He stopped and thought for a moment.

"Are you alright?" Dorothy asked. She could sense his apprehension and became somewhat worried that perhaps Ugu was losing his nerve.

"I'll be fine, Dorothy," he said timidly. "It's just been so long since I've been around other people."

Dorothy handed him a peanut butter sandwich that she had been saving and this seemed to be just the thing to perk up Ugu.

"Thank you, Dorothy," he said in between bites. It had been just the thing he needed to calm his nerves.

They headed towards the approaching town and before long, Ugu and Dorothy found themselves surrounded by the small village and hometown of Ugu the Shoemaker.

The noontime streets of Herku were filled with a great number of people, most of whom were whispering to themselves about the two visitors. Many recognized the old shoemaker and the whispering soon became a chattering of gossip as Dorothy and Ugu moved through the crowds.

"Where's your old shop, Ugu?" Dorothy inquired curiously.

Ugu pointed towards an old, careworn shop at the end of a nearby street.

There, looking as though it were still in business was the old cobbler's shop of Ugu the Shoemaker.

Dorothy and Ugu made their way down the street to the old shop and stood below the sign that hung from the eaves, which read:

Ugu the Shoemaker

Ugu swallowed hard and reached out to turn the old, burnished copper doorknob. The door swung open easily, though a faint creaking sound echoed through the silence of the shop.

Inside, there were various tools hung about on the walls. Tables strewn with cobbler's tools and devices were everywhere. They looked as though they had only been put away just hours ago. The wooden floors were freshly swept and clean.

Just then, a voice sounded out.

"Hello?" inquired the voice from the back room.

Ugu noticed a faint odor of leather that seemed

oddly familiar.

"Anyone here?" Ugu replied. There was a sound of dishes being shuffled and footsteps approached from the back room. Both Dorothy and Ugu held their breath as the door to the back room swung open and a young man appeared.

Standing before Ugu and Dorothy was a blonde-haired young man who appeared to be about twenty five years old.

Dorothy blushed a bit as he was quite handsome in appearance.

His hair was short and well groomed and he had the vibrant appearance of youth. Most noticeable was his lack of shoes, though Dorothy couldn't help but notice his toenails, which were painted a bright, buttercup yellow color. She also noticed a thin, gold chain hung delicately around his right ankle.

"Are you Ugu the Shoemaker?" the young man asked politely.

Both Dorothy and Ugu were taken aback by the young man's question. They nodded in agreement as the young man approached them.

Ugu suddenly began flapping his arms wildly and hopping about the shop and knocking some of the cobbler tools off the nearest table. He made quite a ruckus and screeched loudly at the young man, who seemed quite frightened by the sudden reaction of Ugu.

"Ugu!" shouted Dorothy. "What are you doing?!"

Ugu stopped as quickly as he had begun and did

his best to calm down. He uttered some faint cooing sounds and paced around a bit.

"Please forgive me, Dorothy," Ugu finally managed to say after a few moments. "My old ways as a bird seemed to have taken over there for a moment. I'll be fine in a minute or two."

The young man had also regained his composure after Ugu's frightening display and began picking up the scattered tools and replacing them on the nearby table.

"And who might you be?" Dorothy asked the young man.

"My name is Pacifico," he said confidently.

"And why are you living in my old shop?" Ugu managed to say once he had calmed down.

Pacifico seemed puzzled by Ugu's question. He had been certain that Ugu knew he was coming and Ugu's reaction told him that he did not.

"I received a message from a dragonfly who told me to come here to serve as your apprentice," Pacifico explained. "It was the Tin Woodman who had commanded the dragonfly to deliver his message to me."

Both Dorothy and Ugu looked even more puzzled than before.

"I had once told the Tin Woodman about my desire to be a cobbler when he had visited my village near his Tin Castle," Pacifico continued. "Truly, he must have a heart of gold if he remembered someone like me and my dream to become a cobbler."

Dorothy nodded in agreement. "He does indeed,

though it is actually made of silk and stuffed with sawdust," she replied in earnest.

"So you didn't know I was coming?" Pacifico asked.

"No, I did not," replied Ugu. "But since you're here and since I've been asked to return to my life as a cobbler, having you as an apprentice might be a fine thing indeed. It has been a long time since I've made a pair of shoes."

Pacifico looked as though his fondest wish had come true. He invited Dorothy and Ugu into the back room where he had prepared lunch earlier that morning.

"Is that steamed asparagus?" Ugu asked politely. Despite having eaten peanut butter sandwiches earlier, Ugu found he was quite hungry from the journey.

"Yep! And there's blueberry pie for desert too!" he exclaimed.

"Everyone loves pie!" Dorothy shouted gleefully.

Both Dorothy and Ugu sat down with Pacifico and had their fill of lunch until none could eat no more.

Chapter 18
Margolotte's Enchantment

Mombi had just finished picking her Poppies, placing them in her satchel, and had seen the old woman with the black eye patch passing by in the small boat with the trader.

Even at a distance, she had a vague sense that she knew the old woman, but where from, she couldn't recall.

"Perhaps," Mombi thought to herself, *"she used to practice in the ways of magic just like me?"* She tried hard to recall who the old woman was, but found her memory lacking.

"Once I finish with Dr. Pipt, I believe I'll look up that old woman and discover just who she is..." 'Ol Mombi thought once more, *"but one step at a time, old woman, one step at a time."*

It would be a long day and night before she would reach the lonesome home of Dr. Pipt and his wife, Margolotte. After all, she had a thick, dark, impenetrable forest that would be very hard to navigate for anyone, especially an old woman like herself. And then there was the mountain that waited for her to climb. Upon its flanks was the very forest she dreaded passing through.

"Oh my bones, my aching bones! They just weren't meant to climb up a mountainside covered in a thick, dark forest," she thought to herself as she made her way across the Munchkin countryside towards Dr. Pipt's house. She also realized that she had brought nothing for the pain that would greet her afterwards.

"I hope I can find some sweet violet flowers along the way?" 'Ol Mombi muttered to herself. She thought about how the flowers could be brewed into a tea that was very good at relieving pain. "But they're purple and only grow in Gillikin Country where I live." She let out an aching groan that echoed across the blue prairie grass.

The old woman continued her journey eastward, walking along a very old path that would lead her to the edge of the forest that made its way up the lone mountain in the south of Munchkin Country, where Dr. Pipt lived with his wife, Margolotte.

As she made her way across the blue fields of Munchkin Country, crossing the slowly flowing waters of the Munchkin River by means of a blue stone bridge, she thought about how she would try to persuade Dr. Pipt to help her make the Powder of Life.

"I wonder if he still has a wife?" she thought to herself. *"She could be a problem."* 'Ol Mombi patted the small black satchel containing the Poppy Flowers. *"Then again, maybe not…"*

Late in the day, 'Ol Mombi finally came upon the

edge of the forest that rose up the mountainside where Dr. Pipt lived.

She sat down to rest... and to think.

There would be no sense in walking into the forest at night and she was tired, hungry, thirsty and sore. She made a small campfire from some nearby fallen branches since the temperature had dropped somewhat.

Nearby, the old woman found a small creek with some fish swimming about. After some thought, she gathered up a few rocks and tried her hand at throwing them at the fish in hopes of knocking one out and catching it. Soon, she had a pair of fish laid out on the ground, waiting for the old woman's touch.

'Ol Mombi gathered some large leaves from a nearby bush. She sprinkled some marjoram and sage that she found by the edge of the forest onto the fish, then wrapped each fish in the large leaves and placed them among the very hot rocks that were right beside the flames.

Before the sun had even set, the old woman had herself a fine meal, complete with fresh, cool water from the small creek and even some blackberries from a bush by the water. Soon, she was sound asleep by the fireside, the aching in her bones reminding her that she was still just an old woman.

'Ol Mombi got up the next morning and began walking uphill through the forest, being careful to avoid fallen limbs and branches which might cause her to fall and break a leg.

The Emerald Slippers of Oz

The forest was so dark that at times, it was hard to see anything but a few trees in front of her. By mid-afternoon, she came to a small clearing along the mountainside and saw that the forest became even denser as the mountainside became even steeper.

"Oh my…" she muttered out loud to herself. She sat down to rest and catch her breath. Reaching into her satchel, she brought out some left over fish and finished it off quickly. After a long, refreshing drink, the old woman started the long climb up the path that led up the mountainside through the even darker forest.

For many hours, she trod slowly up the path towards the home of Dr. Pipt and his wife, Margolotte.

At least there was still daylight, but barely so, when she reached the top and found the small home among the gnarled trees and bushes of the forested mountainside.

It was round and painted blue so that the house blended in with the sky above. There were neatly pruned blue trees and blue flowers in abundance about the yard. A nearby garden was filled with beds of blue cabbages, blue carrots, and blue lettuce.

Behind the house were bun-trees, cake-trees and cream-puff bushes, all of which were very well kept.

There were also blue buttercups which gave forth a wonderful blue butter while a row of chocolate-caramel plants provided the sweets needed by the house.

Dividing the flower and vegetable beds were paths of blue gravel which lead eventually to the front door.

The Emerald Slippers of Oz

'Ol Mombi was stunned by the sight of Dr. Pipt's house, especially after such a long and hard climb. She hadn't been there in a very long time and had forgotten just how lovely their home was among the darkness of the surrounding forest.

She looked around, then walked to the back of the house where the old woman soon found Dr. Pipt and Margolotte, picking cream-puffs and filling a silver tray with them.

"Greetings, Dr. Pipt!" shouted 'Ol Mombi, still somewhat short of breath from the journey up the hill. "Remember me?!"

Dr. Pipt recognized 'Ol Mombi immediately and turned to see his wife, Margolotte, scowling at him. She recognized 'Ol Mombi as well and she remembered what the old woman used to be.

Dr. Pipt invited 'Ol Mombi into their home and the three made their way into the large room near the center of the blue house. He had decided to be polite, especially since they almost never received visitors. In fact, he couldn't recall the last time they had any visitors.

As for Margolotte, she looked upon 'Ol Mombi as a former witch and not just an old woman. She wondered *"what the old witch wanted,"* while seating herself by her husband, Dr. Pipt.

The three talked of the old days and there was mention of magic and potions, which made Margolotte very nervous. She remembered how her husband's Liquid of Petrifaction had turned her to marble and only the

107

Wizard of Oz could restore her to Life.

Mombi explained to Dr. Pipt about how she missed having The Powder of Life. She wanted to know if he would help her by making some more of the mysterious, magical powder.

"No," Dr. Pipt explained. "I can no longer make The Powder of Life or even practice magic ever since the Wizard of Oz straightened my limbs so they were no longer crooked and I lost my powers."

Dr. Pipt sighed deeply while Margolotte fidgeted and shifted about nervously in her seat. She looked disapprovingly at him and he shook his head once more.

He knew better than to argue or plead because he loved his wife and did not want to anger her.

Margolotte got up and offered to make some tea and biscuits while Dr. Pipt and 'Ol Mombi continued talking about magic and the old ways.

Soon, Margolotte returned with a tray of biscuits, butter and honey, along with several steaming cups of tea and sat it down on the small table next to the old former witch.

"Oh my! I forgot the blackberry jelly!" she said suddenly. Margolotte walked back to the kitchen, muttering to herself all the while.

"I think I'll grab my pipe too!" Dr. Pipt declared as he grabbed a cup of tea and headed for the domed hall in the back of the house.

'Ol Mombi now found herself alone and her mind quickly thought back to her journey across the blue fields of Munchkin Country and her plans for Dr. Pipt.

She reached into her black satchel and grabbed a Poppy flower, then quickly dipped it into the far cup of tea.

No sooner had Mombi replaced the now-dripping Poppy flower back into the satchel when Margolotte returned with a jar of blackberry jelly and a small butter knife.

The old former witch quickly reached for the near cup of tea which she had not dipped a Poppy flower into.

Dr. Pipt appeared moments later, pipe in one hand, tea in the other and a smile on his face.

Margolotte spread butter and jelly onto three small biscuits and served them all around. She reached down and took a small sip of her still-steaming tea.

'Ol Mombi sipped her tea and smiled as Margolotte grew suddenly drowsy. She watched as the chubby, pleasant-faced woman fell fast asleep and slumped over onto the small table, scattering the teapot and jar of blackberry jelly.

By now, Dr. Pipt realized that something was very wrong with his dear wife, Margolotte.

"What has happened to my wife? What have you done to her?!" he cried in anguish.

Margolotte answered with a long, loud snore that echoed through the small round house.

"She will be fine, she's only sleeping," the old witch replied.

"I can hear that!" exclaimed Dr. Pipt.

"I can waken her anytime I want, but only if you help me regain my powers by making the Powder of Life," 'Ol Mombi said calmly and with great conviction.

Of course, she had no plans to revive Margolotte anytime soon, but Dr. Pipt didn't need to know that. For now, she knew that Dr. Pipt would do whatever she demanded of him… and what she was demanding was The Powder of Life.

Chapter 19
In Search Of Emeralds

"I only got here a couple of days ago," Pacifico had explained. "I cleaned up the shop and waited for you to arrive." Ugu paced about the shop and looked things over. He was impressed with the attention to detail that his new apprentice had displayed. The tools were indeed, bright of edge and sharp as could be. Every square foot of flooring had been swept clean and polished.
The leather had been oiled and rubbed, restored to its natural luster.

"Why the bare feet if you want to be a cobbler?" Ugu finally asked. He could have understood if Pacifico had been a bird like he had. Birds had no need of shoes, but Ugu and his apprentice did… or so he thought.

"I like the feel of the world at my feet," Pacifico explained. "Besides, look at those fine painted toenails! Have you seen a more magnificent sight?"

Dorothy giggled and Ugu snorted at Pacifico's boast. She thought better of showing off her own painted toenails, which were painted a bright emerald green.

Ugu recalled his aviary days and was glad he no longer possessed long, black talons.

The Emerald Slippers of Oz

Dorothy only remained a few hours with Ugu and Pacifico, realizing early on that the two seemed to make a sympathetic pair.

Ugu certainly appreciated the company of a fellow human and Pacifico yearned deeply to eventually become a cobbler himself.

She left the two in deep and earnest conversation about the need for better leather and whether the tools were sharp enough.

For Dorothy, her next stop was a return to the Tin Palace to thank the Tin Woodman for his kindness and generosity of heart.

Ugu was indeed grateful for the company as he had been a grey dove for a long time, or so it seemed, and he was eager to hold his tools once more.

For the next few days, Ugu and Pacifico got to know each other and learn about each other's habits and needs.

Pacifico made an ideal apprentice. He was eager to learn and willing to take orders from Ugu. For him, the chance to realize his dreams of becoming a cobbler made life in the shop fun and easy.

Ugu the Shoemaker also found the days easy going and fun. His new apprentice was both eager and willing to learn. For Ugu, the ways of the cobbler returned to him quickly and before long, he had completed his first pair of shoes in many years.

Despite his best efforts though, Ugu found that Pacifico would not wear shoes under any circumstances.

The Emerald Slippers of Oz

"Never a shoe will these feet see!" he proudly
declared one evening as he and Ugu settled down for the
evening.

Clearly, his apprentice preferred the feel of wood
and soil against his bare feet. It seemed odd to have an
apprentice who never wore shoes, but Ugu decided not to
make an issue of it. Pacifico was showing himself to be
very quick at picking up the tricks of the trade and Ugu
decided that bare feet were the least of his worries.

Soon, the citizens of Herku began trickling back
into his shop, curious to see if Ugu was indeed back to his
old trade. The word soon spread around the small town
that Ugu was making shoes once more and business
picked up quickly.

"Have you thought any about Dorothy's request
for a pair of Emerald Slippers?" Pacifico asked Ugu one
early evening following their meal.

"Yes indeed. In fact, I have thought of nothing else
but the Emerald Slippers," he replied. The idea of making
a pair of slippers for the Ruler of Oz had greatly appealed
to Ugu and he considered the possibilities day after day
until he finally came upon a design and style that he felt
would honor Princess Ozma.

"Pacifico!" Ugu called out one early morning. "I've
decided on a design and I need for you to find me a pair of
emeralds."

Pacifico grew anxious at the prospect of finding a
pair of emeralds. He was certain he would have to visit
Emerald City, something he had never done before… and

The Emerald Slippers of Oz

Ugu had made it clear that Princess Ozma was to "know nothing of theses shoes."

"I'm certain that if you search hard enough, a matched pair of emeralds will find their way to you," Ugu explained earnestly to the rapt attention of Pacifico. "They must be clear, bright and pure."

"What will you do in my absence, Ugu?" Pacifico asked his mentor. "Can you manage without me?" He smiled slyly and Ugu was certain he was kidding him on.

Pacifico went to the bathing room and cleaned his feet for the journey. He added a fresh coat of buttercup yellow polish to his now-clean feet.

"When I get back, I'll have a foot'full of emerald dust!" he declared. Pacifico was nervous, but plainly excited at the prospect of visiting the capitol of Oz. He might even *grab a glimpse of Princess Ozma,* he thought to himself.

"Oz always provides..." Ugu assured his apprentice as he bid him "farewell and good luck."

By mid-morning, Pacifico was on his way eastward towards the emerald green country of Emerald City. By his side were an empty yellow satchel and a water-filled gourd.

Before long, Pacifico was past the far hill and out of sight.

Ugu soon found himself nervous at the thought of being alone in his shop. He had spent so many years alone as a grey dove, but now was back to his former self and the thought of being alone felt odd.

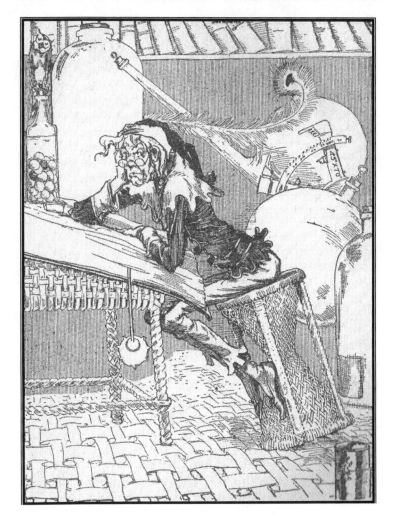

"I wonder how my old nest is doing?" he thought to himself.

Chapter 20
The Back Door

The rest of the day was very tense as 'Ol Mombi and Dr. Pipt argued back and forth about this and that… and even some of the other.

Margolotte snored soundly in the far room on the blue velvet couch.

"I am no longer crooked, as you can plainly see," he shouted while waving his arms and legs about. "Without the crooked limbs, I cannot be a Crooked Magician as I once was. Now, I am only an ordinary Munchkin!"

"Hmmpphh!!" snorted 'Ol Mombi, who was certain that Dr. Pipt would figure out a way now that Margolotte was sleeping so soundly.

The two of them circled about one another, eventually finding a way to share some cheese and fruit juice.

After more stern words and much glaring, the old woman and old man retired to separate rooms to try and get some sleep. Both of them had grown tired from all the anger and angst of the day.

'Ol Mombi slept very lightly that night as she did

not trust Dr. Pipt and what he might do to her.

Dr. Pipt, on the other hand, didn't trust 'Ol Mombi and he had hatched a plan he thought might work.

"We'll head up over the peak and on to the back door," he thought to himself as he lay on his back, sleepless yet exhausted, *"then I'll shove her through and be done with her."*

The former Crooked Magician worried about Margolotte and hoped that 'Ol Mombi didn't hurt her. Her gentle snoring assured him she was alright.

Dr. Pipt was certain however, that 'Ol Mombi had no intention of reviving Margolotte. He had grown to love his wife in leaps and bounds after the lure of magic had been removed long ago. He now loved her even more dearly and felt like he could bring her back from the poison that the old sorceress had used.

"I must make sure to get that bag from her before she goes..." he thought one last time before dozing off.

He felt like he had just closed his eyelids when he heard the old woman rustle around the front room as she fixed hot tea.

A faint glow told him it was near dawn.

"Hot tea..." he thought to himself. *"I wonder what she put in it to make my Margolotte sleep?"*

"Good morning Dr. Pipt," 'Ol Mombi said cheerfully.

"What's so good about it?" he snapped.

"Plenty! You're still alive, aren't you?" she said.

"Yea, if you say so!" he declared.

They drank their tea and had some biscuits and

honey and Dr. Pipt decided to put his plan into action.

He checked in on Margolotte and saw that she slept soundly and peacefully. Knowing this gave him confidence and he puttered about the house for a few minutes, then made his way outside, followed by 'Ol Mombi. They followed a very old path that led from the back of the little blue house on into a very dark forest leading up the mountainside.

"Where are we going?" she asked suspiciously.

"We have to go through the forest and up over the mountain. We will be looking for a cave," he replied, adjusting the pack on his back he had prepared for the journey.

"A cave?" she asked, not quite believing him.

"A cave... just not any old cave but a very special cave that holds magic," Dr. Pipt said in an almost hushed whisper. He had hoped the old woman would be unable to resist... and he was correct.

"How long will this take?" she asked.

"Depends on how fast we go. Usually a few days, give or take," Dr. Pipt suggested confidently.

"A few days!" exclaimed the old woman.

"What's the rush?" he asked in a surprised voice.

"I just thought... nothing," she stammered.

The path was very hard to follow at times and was overgrown with weeds, fallen branches, old roots and such.

On more than one occasion, they had each tripped over the vegetation and after a few hours, 'Ol Mombi sat down to rest and rub her sore feet.

Dr. Pipt watched 'Ol Mombi warily out of the corner of his eye.

"Whatever she poisoned Margolotte with is in that bag," he thought to himself, trying not to stare at it and alert the old woman. He was even more certain now he could produce an antidote to whatever afflicted Margolotte.

After some water from the backpack and a ten minute break, they started walking again at a slow but steady pace

Occasionally, 'Ol Mombi would stop and reach down to examine various different roots, plants and flowers. She grabbed anything that looked useful.

The old woman stopped abruptly, seeing the dark forest rise up even more along the trail they were following uphill.

"You couldn't have found a better way than going through the dark, perilous forest... and uphill to boot?" she inquired with a touch of anger in her voice.

"It can't be helped," replied Dr. Pipt, smirking just a little to himself when her back was turned. He was pleased that she was getting angry and distracted. *"All the easier to dispose of the old hag when the time comes,"* he thought to himself.

Once more, he found himself staring at the little black bag that 'Ol Mombi clutched on to very tightly.

"Let's get going again. We only have a few more hours left, then we'll have to stop for the night," he informed the old woman.

They found several sturdy walking sticks which they hoped would help in the climb up towards the peak.

Soon, the peak of the mountain lay beneath their feet and a small clearing framed the pinnacle of Mount Pipt.

"I could only hope that she might fall down and break a leg," he thought to himself. A moment's reflection cleared the thought from his head. *"No… Then I would have to get her down somehow…"* He couldn't just abandon the old woman… that was just too much for him to even consider.

If only he knew what she had used on his wife, it would have been much easier to concoct a remedy.

"It has to be in that bag," he thought once more.

They made camp on the peak and after a meal of dried fish and some local mushrooms, along with some freshly squeezed juice from a nearby lemon tree, both were soon sound asleep for the night.

Early the next morning, each awoke from their respective nooks on top of Mount Pipt, sore and very tired… but there was no rest for the weary.

Now, the pace of 'Ol Mombi and Dr. Pipt were a bit easier as it was now downhill, along the backside of Mount Pipt, although the route down was as dark as the route up had been.

In the dim light of the trail down, Dr. Pipt continued to agitate 'Ol Mombi as they neared "the back door."

Every once in a while, a squirrel would scamper up a tree, or a deer would leap up and bound away. There was an odd sense of fear among the local populace.

"It was as if Evil had somehow invaded their home and made itself known." Dr. Pipt found himself shaking his head in silent agreement of his own thought.

Suddenly, "the back door" made it appearance along the very narrow trail down, revealing to Dr. Pipt and 'Ol Mombi the entrance to a nicely-sized cave peering out of the side of the mountain.

Dr. Pipt had created "the back door" long ago during his time as the Crooked Magician. It was, in effect, an actual door attached to an opening in the back wall of the cave. The Crooked Magician had been able, by means of his magical skill and talents, to enchant the doorway to take him anywhere within the Land of Oz. He had only used it once before when he had paid a visit to the Merry-Go-Round Mountains. Since that time, he had lost his crooked, magical powers and Margolotte had forbid him from climbing over their mountain in search of "the back door." He had kept that promise until now.

Now, the former Crooked Magician was hoping that Princess Ozma had overlooked his enchanted doorway when She had forbid him to perform any more magic. He was certain he could dispose of the old hag by means of "the back door."

"Is this your magical cave?" 'Ol Mombi asked warily. She sat down on a nearby log to rest her bones and massage her weary feet.

"It's just inside if we hurry!" Dr. Pipt said excitedly, trying his best to entice the old woman into his trap.

"What's the rush?" she asked in a surprised voice.

"I just thought… nothing," he stammered. The old woman seemed bent on resting and Dr. Pipt had wanted her tired and easily subdued when he opened "the back door."

The two not-so-friendly enemies sat there in front of the gaping hole in the side of Mount Pipt for nearly an hour before 'Ol Mombi was ready to see what Dr. Pipt *was really up to.*

As promised, Dr. Pipt led the way into the nicely-sized opening and in the dim light, along the back wall of the cave, stood a large, wooden door, complete with brass hinges and a beautifully ornate, glass doorknob.

As the old man and old woman approached "the back door," the glass doorknob glowed gently blue, infusing the cave with an almost metallic glow.

'Ol Mombi grinned with excitement at seeing the glass doorknob glow blue. She knew magic when she saw it… and this was certainly magic at work.

Dr. Pipt now saw his opportunity and reached out, grasping the glass doorknob and twisting rapidly before thrusting the large wooden door inward.

As he reached out to grab 'Ol Mombi's little black bag, a violent, swirling wind rushed forth from the open hole that lay behind "the back door," and 'Ol Mombi and Dr. Pipt found themselves surrounded by rapidly pulsating tentacles of wind and an onslaught of sound much like a nearby tornado.

Before either one could react, both found themselves sucked out the back of the cave and into the bright light of confusion, mayhem and madness.

Chapter 21
Cold Fish Soup

B y high noon, Pacifico had made excellent time and was now well south of the Merry-Go-Round Mountains and on his way eastward across vast meadows of yellow prairie grass.

He was glad to have avoided the spinning hills that made up the Merry-Go-Round Mountains. The only way through them was to ride along the spinning mountains like spinning tops on the floor, bouncing from one mountain to another until one emerged out the other side. The few times Pacifico had traveled through the Merry-Go-Round Mountains, the experience of it had made his stomach turn over in a most unpleasant way.

This particular road of yellow granite stones was not often used, but very well maintained. Pacifico was grateful for the smooth stones as they felt good on his bare feet. He decided to stop alongside a small pond and rest a bit.

"I wonder if the road of yellow brick I've heard tell of looks anything like this road?" he thought to himself.

Pacifico's small backpack now lay on the ground beside him and a rather large slice of blueberry pie was setting out on the tin plate, sunlight glinting off of the dark blue juices that were very slowly oozing out from one corner.

Pacifico gazed about the yellow countryside and considered his situation. He was thrilled to have spent the last few weeks eagerly toiling away in the shop of Ugu the Shoemaker. He was also especially pleased that Ugu was showing himself to be kind and understanding mentor of shoemaking and the cobbler's trade.

Many a night he had sat by the fireplace, listening to Ugu tell his stories of life as a bird, and how he had become a bird in the first place.

Pacifico thought to ask Ugu about his life prior to his avian transformation, but it was obvious the one time that Pacifico had tried to ask Ugu about it, there was great turmoil in Ugu's eyes.

The young cobbler's apprentice now made quick work of the slice of pie and after a short nap; he found his bare feet once more walking along the smooth yellow stones that led eastward towards the green countryside of Emerald City.

All along the way, Pacifico thought about where he might find a matching pair of emeralds. He had seen emeralds before when he had visited the Tin Palace of Nick Chopper, who everyone knew as the Tin Woodman; Ruler of the Winkie Country.

His only thought was that *"perhaps in Emerald City, they're just lying around, plentiful enough for anyone to come along and just pick them up!"*

Of course, Pacifico had never been to Emerald City

before, so his idea of what Emerald City was like was certain to be a bit over-exaggerated. In fact, Pacifico had never ventured outside of Winkie Country.

He had heard many a tale about Emerald City. There were green glasses everywhere and roads paved with emeralds. It was also the place where Dorothy lived.

The young man with the bare feet and blonde hair had actually met Dorothy once before when she had passed through his small village and spent the night at the mayor's house. He recalled her stories of lions and tigers and bears.

"Oh my!" Pacifico shouted out as he nearly stepped on a passing field mouse. "Excuse me!"

His thoughts returned to the thought of emeralds as the small field mouse scampered away.

"I wonder how Ugu is doing?" he thought to himself.

By day's end, Pacifico was well into the green, lush lowlands that were the Emerald Country of Emerald City. He was camped out by Lake Quad, just outside a small village which served as a trading port for those coming up from the Quadling Country, which was due south.

To the northwest, the sparkling stars and the glow of Emerald City reflected off of the still, black waters of the largest lake in Oz; Lake Quad. It filled the young bare-footed man from the Winkie countryside with great awe and wonderment.

Soon, Pacifico found himself fast asleep beneath the stellar canopy and within earshot of the lapping waters of the lake. His dreams were filled with visions of emeralds and footwear, and all manner of such so that he awoke the next morning, refreshed and full of energy for the hunt.

The next morning, a young girl from the nearby village visited Pacifico when she saw that he was awake and active. In her hands was a bowl of cold fish soup, which she offered to the young man she had just met.

"We saw that you were alone and thought you might wanna share our morning meal?" she asked somewhat timidly.

The smile from Pacifico assured her he was pleased. He accepted the offering and the two talked for a time.

"Do you know where I might find a pair of emeralds?" he asked the young girl. He had just explained to her about his mission from Ugu the Shoemaker, his mentor and teacher.

The young girl shook her head.

"You might try Emerald City… over there," she said while pointing at the ever-present green glow on the north-eastern horizon. "They got shoes there too!"

Pacifico rolled his eyes and chuckled at the young girl's response.

"That's where I be heading anyways!" he replied. "Never been before, so I have no idea what I'll find there. But one thing's for certain… I won't need shoes!"

The young girl joined him in gentle laughter, and then she thought for a moment.

"I went once long ago, but mostly I stay here by the lake where father fishes and mother cooks," she recalled fondly.

Pacifico thanked her and finished his morning meal without hesitation. It was both filling and delicious, or at least that's what Pacifico thought.

The young girl watched Pacifico and seemed very pleased that he had enjoyed her offering.

"I must be off and on my way," he declared following his morning meal. The young man then gathered what few items had been in his backpack and returned them to it.

Pacifico bid the young girl farewell, and she returned the farewell and waved at the young man she had just met only half an hour before.

Before long, the waters of Lake Quad were behind him and the emerald green countryside of Emerald City was sprawled before him.

It was a happy journey for the young apprentice of Ugu the Shoemaker. He whistled a happy tune and thought happy thoughts about emeralds and cold fish soup and the green glow of Emerald City to his north. All the while, Pacifico pondered the task of finding a pair of emeralds as his bare feet trod the smooth stones, step by step.

Pacifico noticed that the stones now had a very slight greenish tinge to them. He also noticed that a mighty river was approaching... or actually that he was approaching the river.

"This must be the Munchkin River that young girl was talking about," he thought to himself. His thoughts returned

to his home and the Winkie River which flowed nearby.

Pacifico had also spent his life near the water's edge, much like the young girl by Lake Quad, although for him, his dreams had been of the cobbler's life, not that of a fisherman like his father.

He did notice that the waters flowed westward, just as they did with the Winkie River. He recalled his father explaining to him once that "one river flows into the lake and another river flows out of it and we live near the one that flows out." He now knew that he was near the one that flowed into the lake.

The green stone pathway now led Pacifico to a large arched stone bridge crossing the slowly flowing waters. A number of people and several animals were crossing at a leisurely pace.

When he reached halfway across the stone bridge, the bare-footed young man stopped and gazed down at the river. He watched as a lone, small boat with two people in it, approached from upriver.

The man in the boat was holding onto a small rudder in back while an old woman, wrapped in a dark shawl looked up at him from the boat deck. He noticed that she had only one good eye, which was her right eye. Her left eye was covered by a black eye-patch and she waved gently at him.

"Have you seen any emeralds lately?" he asked politely as the boat passed beneath his bare feet and under the stone bridge.

Pacifico made for the other side of the stone bridge

and watched as the small boat emerged.

"I haven't seen one since my younger days, a long time ago," the old woman declared, looking up at him.

"Me neither," replied the man on the rudder. He made a slight adjustment to the rudder so that the boat straightened out and pointed downstream.

Pacifico waved as they floated gently downstream. He then continued on across the stone bridge and turned north along the green stone roadway that snaked its way across the lush green countryside. In the distance, the green glow of Emerald City was ever-present.

Chapter 22
Blinkie's Journey Down The River

B linkie and the old man stopped at a small village for the night. It had been hours since they had passed the Poppy Fields and now they were stopped along the border with the Quadling Country and Emerald City Country.

She had been so immersed in her thoughts of the old lady in the Poppy Fields that they had passed and she wondered who the old woman was. Blinkie had tried to recall each witch that she knew and those that she had heard about.

"We be stopping for the night," the old man said, but Blinkie hadn't heard him as she gazed back toward they way they had passed. *"Maybe she had some sort of…"* what was the word he tried to think of *"… must be that concoction she made up for her aching joints that makes her mind slip away,"* he thought.

He got out of the boat and was greeted by a pleasant old feller who came to greet them.

"Good evening trader. Are you staying the night

131

and need a place to sleep?" said the pleasant old feller.

"Yes. She will need a place also," said the old man, pointing back at Blinkie.

"Oh! I thought she was your wife!" the pleasant old feller said embarrassingly.

The old man laughed loudly and even snorted a bit at what he thought was a fine joke.

"No... she just wants to see the countryside," the old man finally admitted after regaining his senses.

"Yes... seeing the countryside is very relaxing," the pleasant old feller agreed.

Just then, Blinkie came out of her trance of thoughts.

"Oh, are we here already?" she inquired. "Good... I need to get up and stretch anyway."

As she stood, her joints creaked and popped so that both men grimaced as they heard the ancient sound.

"If you both would follow me, I can find you some nice accommodations for each of you," the pleasant old feller said pleasantly.

Soon, both were well fed and sleep soon overtook them in their separate accommodations.

Early the next morning, they were once again on their way, stopping briefly to trade for things for the old man's village.

Traveling along the Munchkin River was so relaxing that Blinkie felt much like she had in her younger days of fishing as a child.

By early afternoon, they had stopped at another

small village and got out to stretch and conduct commerce.

She walked around, looking at a particular fruit stand, then some other various stands that the locals had set up for commerce and such.

After a time, she overheard some people talking about Ugu the Shoemaker, who was "now back in Herku, making shoes once again."

"Wasn't he an old wizard who performed magic long ago?" she thought to herself. *"I wonder if he still does now?"*

People were talking excitedly about how good he had been and still was at making shoes, especially unique-looking shoes.

"Wasn't he once that wizard that had kidnapped Princess Ozma and turned Her into a Golden Peach Pit?" someone had declared.

"Yes he was, and I remember, didn't Dorothy defeat him somehow?" another asked.

"Yes, she did! Pretty little thing from some place called Kansas..." Blinkie recalled. She remembered Dorothy, who was a friend of the Scarecrow.

The old woman shivered at the thought of the Scarecrow, remembering how he had defeated her long ago.

"Ready to go now?" the old man asked Blinkie as she jumped nervously. "Sorry! Didn't mean to scare you."

He shoved off with much waving and smiles from the locals and soon, they were heading down the river towards Lake Quad.

A few hours later, they came upon the fairly large

village of Quadeast, which borders the eastern shore of Lake Quad; where the Munchkin River enters the lake.

The old man excused himself to conduct trade and commerce while Blinkie ventured about the old lakeside village.

Soon, Blinkie overheard the locals talking about Ugu the Shoemaker once again.

A local woman showed off the great shoemaker shoes that he had made "years and years ago!"

After a time, the talk of Ugu subsided as other topics of interest took hold of the locals.

Blinkie didn't hear anything more of interest and walked around aimlessly. She soon found an old tree trunk that had been smoothed down into a seat and rested her weary bones.

Looking down at her swollen feet, she happened to notice a 6-leaf clover standing alone in a patch of moss.

"Odd..." she thought. "A 6-leaf clover is supposed to posses magic... Magic? Yes! That's right..."

The old woman looked around quickly before she carefully picked it and put it quickly in her new black bag.

"I will find a use for that..." she thought as she got up to stretch.

Blinkie nervously started walking back to the boat and got in when she reached it.

The old man was also ready to head out just as she was.

They could both see the glow of Emerald City off in the distance to the north and Blinkie hunkered down more deeply into the seat in the boat.

"Are you cold?" the old man asked her when he had seen her shiver.

"Just a tad bit..." she replied.

"There is a spare blanket under your seat to cover with," he suggested as he rowed the boat out and onto the immense body of water that was Lake Quad. On the other side and a bit upriver was the home of the Scarecrow and Blinkie's fear was becoming quite apparent.

Soon, all sight of land was lost and the small boat and its occupants were surrounded by blue waters and the ever-present green glow of Emerald City to the northeast.

"Are you getting' sick?" the old man asked her gently.

"I don't know... I feel a little warm to the touch, so perhaps when we stop again I'll brew up something," she replied as she glanced once again toward the west where she knew the Scarecrow's home was. *"I have to get myself south of here and soon before anybody recognizes me."* She thought and shivered.

Toward the evening, as the far western coast of Lake Quad came into view, the old man announced that they would stop for the night at the town of Quadwest, which lay at the mouth of the Winkie River; which flowed into Winkie Country.

"By tomorrow noon, we'll be at the home of the Scarecrow, where I do my best business!" declared the old man.

Blinkie recalled the place where the Scarecrow

called home. It appeared exactly like a very large ear of corn, complete with rooms, halls, and all manner of interior furnishings.

"Oh!" she said suddenly. "I'll be getting off at Quadwest... if you don't mind?" Blinkie said somewhat timidly. She had no desire to be anywhere near the home of the one who had so defeated her so long ago. She had never forgot being shrunk to less than half her original size before being stripped of her magic powers and restored to full height.

The old man was quite puzzled as to why the old woman suddenly needed to depart his ship. However, he obliged Blinkie and made for port in Quadwest with great haste.

Soon, the small boat was tied up in dock and Blinkie made to step back onto dry land after the daylong trip across Lake Quad.

"Thank you for your kindness, dear sir," she spoke clearly. "Too much noise and excitement get to me after a while. Besides, I need to brew something for this cold and fever and perhaps take a day or two of rest before moving on."

The old man lent Blinkie his hand and helped her across the gangplank and onto the firm, yellow soil of Winkie Country and the dockside village of Quadwest.

Chapter 23
The Merry-Go-Round Mountains

D r. Pipt and 'Ol Mombi now found themselves in what could only be described as controlled chaos. The doorway through which they had passed led to a point just above and directly in the middle of the Merry-Go-Round Mountains.

Row upon row of cone-shaped mountains surrounded the odd couple now caught in the middle. Each mountain spun rapidly upon its axis, each opposite to its next door neighbor so that Dr. Pipt and 'Ol Mombi were bounced back and forth between opposing peaks, spinning this way and that way, neither of them able to remain motionless and stationary.

"I forgot about how these things work," Dr. Pipt thought to himself. The swirling winds that had drawn him and the old woman into the midst of the Merry-Go-Round Mountains had been far stronger than he had remembered. They made a loud, rushing sound and he could barely hear himself think.

The Emerald Slippers of Oz

As he bounced back and forth, Dr. Pipt lost sight of 'Ol Mombi among the spinning peaks. He cursed himself for his failed plan and wondered how Margolotte was doing.

As for 'Ol Mombi, she was equally stunned by the sudden situation she now found herself in. She clutched tightly onto her little black bag and spun about in tight little circles as she leapt from mountain to mountain, much like a small ball might bounce about between a flock of spinning tops.

Over and over and head over heels she spun, her head spinning nearly as fast as her old bones were going at the moment.

'Ol Mombi tried to keep track of Dr. Pipt but soon lost sight of him as she spun to and fro, back and forth between spinning peak after spinning peak.

She thought back to a story she heard long ago about how Dorothy and her little dog Toto had once traveled through the spinning menagerie of mountain peaks.

"No wonder she was such a silly little girl," the old woman thought to herself. *"Only a silly little girl could find this of any fun!"*

Suddenly, 'Ol Mombi felt herself thrust forward through several spinning mountain peaks towards what looked like a large grove of trees. From the corner of her eye, 'Ol Mombi could see the canopy of leaves between the

139

spinning mountains; though she wasn't quite certain as she herself was spinning madly like an out-of-control top.

Just then, the whirling surface beneath her spat the old woman out and sent her tumbling through the great grove of trees and on past towards a high wall standing in the distance.

'Ol Mombi came to a sudden halt, stopped by the high wall of wood and copper that towered far above the old woman.

Just then, Dr. Pipt came following along to a screeching halt not more than two or three feet from the old woman. He too had been deposited by the Merry-Go-Round Mountains at the foot of the high wall. The only problem was that Dr. Pipt seemed to have been bound up into a tight little ball. His arms and legs appeared to have been splayed about his body so that they assumed a most unusual position. It was as though his limbs had been rearranged, much like a rubber doll might be, only in very unnatural positions.

It took the old woman several minutes to regain her senses and stop the whole of Oz from spinning about in her mind.

Dr. Pipt meanwhile, had taken to yelling for help, though his cries were somewhat muffled by the fact that his right leg had wrapped around his head, covering his mouth for the most part.

'Ol Mombi looked him over and could see that his left arm was bent back around his backside while his left leg and right arm had found themselves wrapped around his upper waist.

Whatever he had planned for her had failed... and she was glad of it.

Chapter 24
Emerald City

Pacifico stared up at the massive green marble columns that served as the Southern Gate into Emerald City.

Peeled back from the massive columns were two immense wood and bronze doors, which stood perpetually open for all to enter. They were studded with all manner and sizes of emeralds, all of which were formed into a large OZ symbol on each door.

Atop the massive columns were two very large, expertly cut emeralds, both glowing brightly, even in the sunlight.

The young bare-footed man with blond hair and a thin gold chain strung gently about his right ankle stood dumbstruck by the sight of the Southern Gate.

People streamed by him as he stood there and marveled at the immensity of it all. The doors alone were bigger than even those at the Tin Palace of the Tin Woodman.

In the distance were the tall spires and domes of Emerald City, all aglow in a soft, green radiance that seemed to bathe everyone walking about in a very faint, green iridescence.

The Emerald Slippers of Oz

Everywhere were all manner of people in all manner of dress and décor. There was a general buzz of excitement and occasional shouts from friends as they greeted each other. The old city was alive and kicking and the local populace, along with its many visitors, seemed to call out to the young man on a mission.

Pacifico looked down at his bare feet and saw that the buttercup yellow of his toenails were quite faded and peeling. The journey had been hard on his feet, even with the gentleness of the stone roadways leading through Oz.

"I should' a brought some polish with me?" he thought to himself.

No sooner had the thought crossed his mind when two young ladies appeared from a nearby doorway and curtsied before him.

"We see you are new to Emerald City and welcome you warmly!" exclaimed the two young ladies in unison. They kneeled down and before the stunned young man of blonde hair could say anything, they had begun to paint his toenails with a bright, emerald green polish.

Pacifico stood there, amazed at how quickly the two young ladies worked at their task. He noticed that both girls were dressed in green gingham and matching green shoes and both sported flaming red hair in flowing ringlets.

Moments later, both young ladies stood up and shook Pacifico's hand, smiling at him and walking back into the nearby doorway from whence they had so abruptly appeared.

143

The Emerald Slippers of Oz

Pacifico was very pleased with the new look of his now bright emerald green toenails. He could tell that there was emerald dust sparkling throughout the coating on his toenails.

"I did tell Ugu I would come back with emerald dust on my feet... I just didn't think it would be like this," he thought to himself.

Pacifico snapped his fingers as he realized that he had not asked the two young ladies about emeralds.

"Well, there's plenty of people around to ask," he said to himself under his breath. There were indeed a great number of people milling about the green marble sidewalks and various shops of Emerald City. More people, in fact, than Pacifico had ever seen before in one place. The large, green marble facades dotted here and there were unlike anything he had ever seen before, though he seemed to be the only one dumbfounded by the sight of Emerald City.

He sat down on a nearby bench and propped one foot up on his knee to catch his breath and examine the handiwork of the Emerald City greeting.

As Pacifico moved to set his foot down on the green marble below the bench, he caught sight out of the corner of his eye a flash of brown and heard a faint squeak as he quickly lifted his foot to avoid stepping on whatever was just underfoot.

"Excuse me!" Pacifico exclaimed as he saw the little brown field mouse scurry away. "I beg your pardon!"

Pacifico felt relief at not having harmed the little

mouse. He remembered having nearly stepped on one several days before and was just as glad then not to have hurt the little creature.

"You look like a man on a mission," inquired a local citizen of Emerald City.

Pacifico looked up and saw a jovial man of about fifty years of age with an emerald green moustache and matching hair. His clothing, along with the hair and moustache told Pacifico that this must be a local citizen.

"I am indeed!" Pacifico exclaimed. He then explained his mission to the man, who listened politely and with great attention. "Would you know where I could find a fine pair of emeralds for my master's work?"

"I cannot say for I do not know," replied the jovial man. "They don't grow on trees and all the emeralds here in Emerald City serve their own purpose on behalf of Princess Ozma. Perhaps you could ask Her for a pair of emeralds?"

Pacifico hadn't mentioned who Ugu was making the shoes for and he figured asking the Princess would spoil the whole surprise for Dorothy.

"Perhaps..." he said, though not with much enthusiasm.

The jovial man excused himself and headed towards the center of the old city.

Pacifico asked citizen after citizen, visitor after visitor... and even several animals who had returned his greetings to them.

"I have no idea where you might find a pair of

emeralds just lying about," said the Cowardly Lion, who happened to be visiting Emerald City that day.

Pacifico had no idea that he was addressing the King of all the animals of Oz. To the bare-footed young man of blonde hair and the thin gold chain, the Cowardly Lion was just a big cat he had met today. In fact, He was the first big cat Pacifico had ever met, though Pacifico had met other smaller animals before and so wasn't really surprised by a talking lion.

He had nearly drunk from the Forbidden Fountain in the center of Emerald City when a local woman offering loaves of bread to passerby's warned him of the effects of the water from the fountain.

"You best be careful or you'll wind up with

nothing but an empty head and no more dreams," she warned. "Even a single drop will cost you a day's memories." The woman offered him some water from a pouch hanging from her belt, as well as a loaf of bread, which the young man accepted gratefully.

By day's end, Pacifico had exhausted himself from scouring the old city for a pair of emeralds to fulfill Ugu's request.

Now, Ugu's apprentice sought a place for the night as he was quite fatigued from the day's adventure.

His search didn't take long as there were plenty of choices around, all of which were far nicer than any place he had bedded down during his journey from Herku.

Chapter 25
The Gemini Emeralds

T he next morning, Pacifico awoke, refreshed and eager to continue his search for the perfect pair of emeralds for Ugu's needs. A quick meal in the inn where he had spent the night and Pacifico was once more scouring the old city for a matching pair of emeralds just lying about.

By mid-morning, Pacifico had reached the other side of Emerald City and he thought he might never find what he was looking for. No one he had spoken to had any idea where spare emeralds might be found.

Just then, a small, green and black dragonfly buzzed about Pacifico's head, examining him and flitting about the young man.

"It is you!" the green and black dragonfly exclaimed in a very small voice. "I have been looking for you all morning!"

Pacifico cocked his head to one side and wondered about the small insect that was now talking to him. The dragonfly was hard to hear and Pacifico couldn't imagine why the little insect was looking for him.

"Her Majesty, the Queen of the Field Mice requests the honor of your presence at Her residence in the south fields of Emerald Country," the green and black dragonfly declared faintly. "Please follow me!"

Pacifico shook his head in disbelief. He was unsure

148

if the green and black dragonfly was serious or not, but since he had not found a single emerald lying about, let alone a pair of them, Pacifico decided that perhaps a visit to the home of the Queen of the Field Mice might make a nice change of pace.

"Besides, "he thought to himself, *"I'm not finding anything here anyways."*

Pacifico followed behind as the green and black dragonfly flew through the throngs of people and animals milling about the old city until they passed through the Southern Gate and were headed away from the Emerald City. He kept thinking about Ugu and how he was going to explain just how he was unable to locate even a single loose emerald in Emerald City.

"Keep up, keep up!" declared the green and black dragonfly as he buzzed the blonde hair of Pacifico. "We mustn't keep Her waiting!"

After about an hour or so of walking south, the green and black dragonfly turned east and headed directly into a large green meadow. Pacifico followed along for another hour as they made their way across the lush green vegetation of the meadow into a field of prairie grasses.

Soon, a small hill appeared in the distance and the green and black dragonfly became very excited as they approached the home of the Queen of the Field Mice.

When they reached the small hill, the green and black dragonfly buzzed about excitedly while Pacifico looked around. All he could see was lush green sawgrass covering the small hill.

The Emerald Slippers of Oz

In the distance behind them, the glow of Emerald City was still quite visible, although none of even the tallest spires of the old city were seen.

Pacifico wondered what he was doing standing in the middle of a field.

"Well, I can always tell Ugu that I was out standing in my field," he said out loud.

There was a very faint groan from the surrounding prairie grass of the small hill.

Suddenly, the ground at his feet seemed to come alive as hundreds of field mice scampered about, surrounding the young man of blonde hair and forming a large circle around him. A number of mice scurried across his bare feet, causing Pacifico to laugh out loud as their little paws tickled his toes.

No sooner had the mice all come to a complete standstill when the Queen of the Field Mice came scampering out of a small hole near the top of the small hill.

Although She appeared nearly like every other mouse now standing at attention in a large circle surrounding the Queen's invited guest, Pacifico could tell by the way She approached him and the way She carried Herself that this particular rodent was royalty... that and the small gold crown She wore on Her head.

"Your Majesty, I'm told you wanted to see me?" Pacifico said inquisitively as he bowed before the Royal Monarch of all the mice in Oz. He knew very well that, be they man or mouse, a person of royalty always commanded respect and courtesy.

"Indeed I did," She replied. Her voice was both regal and confident in tone and Pacifico rose to face the Queen of the Field Mice.

Of course, he then had to kneel down in order to address Her Majesty more politely as he seemed to tower over all the mice in the kingdom surrounding him. Pacifico could see in Her eyes a kind and benevolent Ruler; one who truly cared for Her subjects and ruled with compassion and kindness.

Such is the reign of the Queen of the Field Mice.

"It has come to My attention that you have shown a kindness and compassion to not one, but two of My subjects these last few days," She declared, Her voice now commanding and royal, "and I am disposed to grant you a wish."

All of the field mice squeaked and scurried about in harmonious joy at the Queen's proclamation.

Pacifico thought back over the last few days and wondered which subjects the Queen was referring to. He had only seen two field mice since his journey to Emerald City began and he hadn't done any kindness to them that he could recall.

"Which subjects are Your Majesty referring to?" he inquired.

"In the Winkie Country, on the road leading into Emerald Country, you nearly stepped on my Royal Messenger, Millicent Mouse, but showed great compassion and kindness in your efforts to spare her harm," the Queen explained as She motioned towards a small brown field mice who appeared to be waving happily at Pacifico.

"And in Emerald City, your compassion and kindness showed itself once again when you avoided harming my Royal Nephew, Milo Mouse… and even showed great remorse, as any kind person would do." She motioned to another field mouse who appeared very much like all the other mice surrounding them.

"When I received word of your valor, I sent my good friend to find you and bring you to Me," the diminutive mouse explained.

Just then, the green and black dragonfly came buzzing along, flitting here and there as he looked for a place to land.

"It was my pleasure, Your Majesty," declared the green and black dragonfly from his perch on the tall blade of prairie grass near the Queen of the Field Mice.

"Thank you, Cordulia!" She exclaimed. The green and black dragonfly flew off to a chorus of cheers from the assembled field mice and vanished in the distance of the gently waving prairie grass.

"And now for you, My dear!" the Queen of the Field Mice declared as She turned Her attention to Pacifico. "What wish might I grant for you? What dream are you chasing, kind sir?"

Pacifico now poured his heart out to the assembled legion of field mice and their Queen. He explained about his desire to be a shoemaker and his mission to find a matching pair of emeralds for his mentor, Ugu the

Shoemaker.

Remembering what Ugu had told him, he had once again failed to mention who the Emerald Slippers were for.

Pacifico spoke of his journey across Oz; his search through Emerald City and all the people and animals he had met during his journey.

The Queen of the Field Mice listened patiently and could easily tell how important Pacifico's mission was to him. Knowing this made Her decision all that much easier for the diminutive little mouse with the small gold crown on Her head.

"So it's a matching pair of emeralds for which you seek, is it?" She proclaimed. "Very well!" Bring forth the Gemini Emeralds!!!"

The throngs of field mice gathered about now scurried here and there with great excitement and joy. A number of mice vanished into the nearby hole in the small hill and emerged a few minutes' later, carrying two large, rectangular emeralds. Pacifico couldn't help but notice that each emerald was larger than any mouse present in the field. In fact, it took several mice to carry each emerald from their cache in the small hilltop back to the Queen of the Field Mice.

The Queen admired the emeralds as they made their way towards Her. The sunlight glinted off the bright green surface of each precious gem, sparkling brightly and showering the assembled mice with bright shafts of green sunlight.

The Queen now turned Her attention to the bare-footed young man of blonde hair and a thin gold chain about his right ankle.

She explained that the Gemini Emeralds had been a gift to Her long ago from Dorothy Gale of Kansas after the Queen of the Field Mice and Her subjects had saved the Cowardly Lion from the deadly Poppy Fields nearby. The Queen also explained that, being so large, She had been unable to find a use for the Gemini Emeralds. She was very pleased now to finally find someone for who they would find a good purpose.

"In honor of your kindness and compassion to My subjects, I present to you, the Gemini Emeralds. May they serve your mentor's needs," the Queen of the Field Mice proclaimed. "And remember these words of advice."

At this, the throngs of mice got suddenly very quiet.

"Chase every dream no matter how small,
you'll have loads of fun but you won't catch them all,
and when you do find that your dream has come true,
you'll find that it always was there inside you."

Suddenly, the throngs of mice erupted in cheers and squeaks of joy. The ground was abuzz with scurrying mice and Pacifico bowed deeply before the Queen as he gathered up the Gemini Emeralds.

"Good day and may your dreams always come true!" proclaimed the Queen of the Field Mice.

The Emerald Slippers of Oz

No sooner had She made Her declaration when every mouse within sight suddenly made for cover, leaving Pacifico alone among the gently waving sawgrass of the southern fields of Emerald Country.

The bare-footed young man of blonde hair and the thin gold chain on his right ankle looked down at his bright, emerald green toenails, then he gazed happily at the two large, expertly cut, rectangular emeralds sitting in his hand.

He laughed softly, shook his head in disbelief, then turned westward and made for Herku and his mentor, Ugu the Shoemaker.

Chapter 26
Journey To Herku

B linkie watched as the old man and his small boat rounded the bend in the Winkie River and vanished from view. The sun was getting low, but the old man had insisted he could make the Scarecrow's Dock before dark.

She would miss the old man in the boat as she had somewhat enjoyed his company, in so much as she could enjoy anyone's company after being alone for so long.

She found a small stream that fed off a larger pond which had formed nearby. The old woman quickly grabbed a fish that had ventured into a shallow spot. It shook violently in her grasp, but the old woman held on as though her life depended on it. Being her evening meal, it did.

After grabbing enough wood and making a small fire, she then cooked up a fine dinner with a strong brew of sassafras tea. The old woman added some of her own plants from her satchel that she thought would calm her jittery nerves. She shivered again with the thought of the nearby Scarecrow.

With the dockside town of Quadwest nearby, Blinkie bedded down on some moss by an old stump.

Before long, sleep overtook her as thoughts of her fine meal and the impending journey on her own tomorrow filled her withered old head.

Blinkie had decided to seek out Ugu the Shoemaker before the old man and his small boat had even crossed Lake Quad the day before.

Now, she aimed her sights at Herku and if she found that old woman she saw in the poppy fields, that would be great too.

Blinkie woke up fresh and relaxed and ready to start the day after stretching and popping her old bones.

After filling up an old small jug with fresh water for her journey alone, she grabbed the sturdy walking stick that she had found the evening before while gathering wood.

Blinkie set off, away from the dockside village of Quadwest in the general direction in which she thought would be Herku. Fortunately, there was a smooth cobblestone road of pale gray that led the way.

With her one good eye occasionally looking down at the ground for more plants, roots, or anything that she could use for magic, the old woman let herself daydream of magic as she slowly ambled along towards the East along the gray cobblestone path.

She found a most interesting flower that she picked and added to her ever-growing supply of flowers, herbs and roots.

Blinkie stopped and checked to see that her 6-leaf clover was safely tucked away in the inner pocket reserved for her valuables, of which she had none, save for the clover leaf.

She thought again of the old lady she had seen picking those red flowers and wondered about her.

"I know I know her…" she thought pensively. *"I just know I know her… but from where, I just don't know."*

At noon, the old woman stopped again and ate some fresh berries that she had found along a yellow picket fence.

"I must be in Winkie Country now" the old woman muttered out loud.

The berries proved to be a very good snack for Blinkie… not too much nor too little, but just enough to settle an empty stomach.

She saw a young couple heading toward her and they were very engrossed in a conversation.

"Good day to you," the young woman said when she saw Blinkie sitting on a large yellow rock.

"Good day to you too," Blinkie replied.

"Have you heard about Ugu the Shoemaker?" the young woman asked excitedly.

Before Blinkie could answer, the young man offered his reply.

"Just that people say he's making shoes again," he said plainly, as though both the young woman and Blinkie already knew.

"Well that he is," the young woman replied. "But I heard that Dorothy has asked him to make a pair of shoes for Princess Ozma."

Blinkie had not heard this before during her travels

along the river.

"A pair of shoes? For her? Why her?" Blinkie asked as she felt a headache and a great unease coming on suddenly. The old woman couldn't seem to understand why the Ruler of Oz would need an ordinary pair of shoes. Certainly, shoes were the least of Princess Ozma's needs.

"I don't know… but they say he sent his apprentice in search of something…" the young woman suggested.

"You don't say?" Blinkie asked.

"Yes… and…" the young woman started to say. She hesitated and looked around.

"And what?" Blinkie exclaimed, nearly jumping from her seat on the large yellow rock.

Just then, the young man leaned in and motioned both woman towards him.

"They say that Mombi has been seen wandering about," he said in a hushed and fearful whisper. "The thought of former witches wandering about again is making people edgy. Can you imagine what is going on? People are getting really nervous."

Both the young man and young woman looked at each other in unspoken understanding.

"Well, we must be on our way. We are heading home after being gone for a few weeks. Where are you headed?" the young woman said innocently.

Blinkie tried to think of something quick and harmless.

"Herku… Just going to see the countryside and Herku is my next stop," the old woman said calmly. It was the truth, though Blinkie conveniently forgot to mention that she was looking for Ugu the Shoemaker.

"Oh... Well good luck and stay clear of any witches!" the young woman exclaimed. Both her and Blinkie laughed, although Blinkie's laugh was not quite genuine.

"Of course..." came the old woman's reply.

Once again, Blinkie started walking eastward, though her pace had quickened just a bit. She looked behind her from time to time to make sure the Scarecrow wasn't sneaking up on her.

As darkness came upon the old woman, she stopped for the evening by a small brook and found refuge under a weeping willow tree. She ate some cold fish that she had saved from her last catch and then laid down to sleep.

The next morning was a bit chilly, but Blinkie had a small fire going in no time. She wrapped herself in her old shawl and made a strong brew of peppermint tea, which greatly warmed her up.

Soon, the fire was extinguished and Blinkie was walking once more.

She was getting close to Herku as she could see more and more people walking along the smooth cobblestone pathway, which was now a pale yellow color.

After a few stops and rests, she finally came upon a large wall which led to an even larger gate of burnished copper, and Blinkie knew she had finally reached Herku.

As she stood there, impressed by the sunlight

glinting off of the burnished copper, Blinkie looked around and found herself face-to-face with an old woman and an old man, both of whom didn't look too happy.

The old man also looked as though he had been crumpled up like a wad of paper and then hastily unscrambled. His arms and legs appeared to go in every direction but the right ones.

Blinkie then looked back at the old woman and quickly realized that she had seen the old woman before. She was the old woman who Blinkie had seen *"picking those pretty red flowers."*

Suddenly, it dawned on Blinkie who the old woman was standing before her.

Chapter 27
The Four Former
Conjurers of Magic

U gu the Shoemaker looked up from his workbench and noticed that customers had entered his humble cobbler's shop. He wished now that Pacifico had never left, for the constant stream of customers had permitted him hardly any time at all for actually making shoes. It would seem that people were glad he was back to work making shoes.

Ugu got up and greeted the new customers, none of whom he ever seen before in his shop.

"Welcome! Welcome! Please enter and tell me your needs!" exclaimed Ugu in a familiar and well-practiced tone. He walked about the three customers as each one eyed the old shoemaker warily.

"You be Ugu…? Ugu the Shoemaker?" asked the old woman in the black shawl with the black satchel by her side. She had the look of having been around Oz a very long time.

"If the sign above the door is correct, then I be Ugu!" replied the old shoemaker.

The Emerald Slippers of Oz

The old woman in the black shawl snorted and
looked around the shop.

"How can I be of…" Ugu started to ask the man
who looked to Ugu like he had been caught in a
whirlwind. The man had arms and legs as crooked as any
he had seen… Ever! He almost appeared to be walking on
his hands, while at other times; his legs looked to be
reaching out to grasp something.

"We heard tell you make the finest shoes in Oz?"
asked the crumpled up, crooked-limbed man.

"That's what I'm told, kind sir… but I can't tell
from looking at you which are your hands and which are
your feet!" replied Ugu. "I would have a hard time
deciding if I should make shoes or gloves for you."

The other old woman in the black shawl chuckled
at Ugu's pun, then cleared her throat.

"Ahem…" she coughed.

Ugu looked the other old woman up and down and
noticed something unmistakable. She had only one good
eye, if the black eye patch over her left eye was any clue.
She too clutched a black satchel by her side.

"I've come for a very special reason, and if my
hunch is correct, these two here are here for the same
reason," the other old woman said calmly. She
remembered seeing the old woman in the Field of Poppies,
gathering flowers only a few days ago. Blinkie had finally
recognized the old woman traveling with the man who
was all crooked and crumpled up when they met at the
gates of Herku. She was now more certain of it when all

three of them headed for the same old shop on the far side of town.

As the former Queen of all the witches in Jinxland, a southern province of Quadling Country in the south of Oz, Blinkie had known every witch under her rule… and many of the other witches of Oz. She recalled Mombi as being nearly as powerful as she had once been. She also recalled that the old witch had been defeated long ago by Glinda; Good Witch of the South and Ruler of the Quadling Country of southern Oz.

Blinkie had been unsure as to who the crooked, crumpled up man was traveling with 'Ol Mombi. He had remained silent ever since their meeting at the gates.

Then, it suddenly dawned on her who he might be.

"This here's Mombi, an old crone from Gillikin Country, far to the north," explained Blinkie as she pointed at the old woman standing next to her.

'Ol Mombi snorted once more, then looked away as Ugu directed his gaze at her.

"Is she right?" he asked the old crone.

Mombi glared at Blinkie, then slowly nodded her head.

"And you are?" Ugu asked the old woman with the one good eye.

"She's Blinkie, an old hag from down south in Jinxland!" exclaimed 'Ol Mombi.

Blinkie snorted much like 'Ol Mombi had done. She shuffled about, then nodded her head when Ugu asked her to confirm 'Ol Mombi's claim.

166

The Emerald Slippers of Oz

"And who might you be?" Ugu inquired of the silent man with the crooked limbs.

"Dr. Pipt!" replied the two old women in unison.

Ugu backed away a few steps and found an old wooden stool upon which he quickly sat down. The old shoemaker knew exactly who each one of his visitors had been and how they had lost their powers.

It would seem that a cobbler's shop heard all the gossip and rumor than ran rampant across Oz and all this he had known before he ever became a grey dove.

He recalled Mombi's defeat at the hands of Glinda; how Blinkie had been conquered by none other than the Scarecrow... and then there was Dr. Pipt.

Ugu knew well the Powder of Life, for he had known several creations which had been given Life by the powder that the once-crooked magician called Dr. Pipt had created.

As a grey dove, Ugu recalled seeing an odd contraption with four wooden legs attached to a large box with a large golden horn, running about the countryside. He recalled that it played music, though not very good music to his ears and he had heard that it had been brought to Life by the Powder of Life... and yet, it was all so long ago.

Ugu walked over to the front door, took the "closed" sign from the back of the door and hung it on the front of the door.

In Oz, it seems, no secret is safe, no matter how hard one tries to keep it.

167

The Emerald Slippers of Oz

For the next several hours, Dr. Pipt, 'Ol Mombi and Blinkie explained to Ugu their desire to return to the old ways of magic, even in defiance of Princess Ozma. Each of them also knew that Ugu had once been a very powerful sorcerer himself.

The old shoemaker sat there, listening to every detail while recalling his years as a great magician long ago. All thoughts of shoemaking, his former life as a grey dove and even his defeat at the hands of Dorothy, who had been the one to transform him into the grey dove, left his mind.

In time, he too felt the allure of magic returning to his thoughts and Ugu soon felt overwhelmed by the desire to perform magic once again.

"Remember, tell no one who we are," warned Blinkie. "There is much talk about wandering sorcerers and witches and we wouldn't want to be accused of being one of them, now would we?"

A cackle of laughter ran through the two former witches while Dr. Pipt grunted a bit. His thoughts returned to his wife, Margolotte, who was still sleeping soundly in their house on Mount Pipt back in Munchkin Country. He was certain that he couldn't trust either one of the old women... and now, he found himself in the company of yet another old magician from long ago. Still though, the thought of regaining his magical powers percolated in the back of his mind.

Just then, the door to the shop creaked open and all four former conjurers of magic turned about to see a young man with blonde hair and a thin gold chain wrapped around his right ankle walking into the cobbler's shop of Ugu the Shoemaker.

Chapter 28
Emerald Dreams

Green clouds crashed together, spilling out in a cascade of vapor and liquid and green ice crystals across vividly blue skies. Swirls of green vapor spun about in casual meanderings across the landscape of Oz.

A low hum invaded the senses as more mist appeared from beyond view, rolling in like a wave from a green sea. It grew slightly in intensity as the mist parted, revealing more clouds of green rolling headlong across the low slung prairie grasses that ran for as far as the eye could see.

It was as though suddenly, an orchestra had been flung about across the countryside and each member had played on whenever possible, though all without direction. There was a crescendo of madness washing over the misty fields as flashes of green lightning ran amok across the prairie fog.

Waves of small creatures skittered among the prairie grass and dense thickets, dancing around the swirling mists and vapors of the green, all the while dodging the thunderbolts of Oz.

In a sudden flash, the mist parted once more to

170

reveal two piercing green eyes jutting out from the bone-white bird skull and staring out into the darkness beyond.

Dorothy awoke with a start and saw that the Great Sun of Oz was just rising.

"Oh my goodness!" she exclaimed. The muted sounds of shuffling feet and worried voices told her she had aroused the attention of the servant girls who served the Palace of Princess Ozma.

The dream had startled Dorothy and now two young girls had entered the bedroom to insure that Dorothy was unharmed and in no peril.

"I'm fine," Dorothy assured each servant girl who asked how she was. It took several more minutes for Dorothy to find herself alone once again.

Clearly, she was upset at such a vivid dream, but Dorothy was more concerned about its meaning. One of the many things she had learned after many years living in Oz was the power and meaning of dreams.

It was the image of the bird skull that had bothered her most for she knew that it had to represent Ugu the Shoemaker.

"But what can it mean..." she thought to herself.

Following a light breakfast, Dorothy decided to venture out of Emerald City to meet with a good friend of hers who she had first met on her first journey to Oz. Dorothy was certain that the little creatures she had seen in her dream could be found south of Emerald City in the vast fields of prairie grass that surround the old city.

Chapter 29
Peppermint and Chamomile Tea

"Ahhh, this is Pacifico, my apprentice. Did you find what I sent you for?" Ugu asked the young man as he stood there, gaping at the three strangers in the room.

"Uhh, uh, hmmm... yes," he stuttered. "I found two perfect emeralds for your..." Pacifico hesitated. He remembered Dorothy's request to remain quiet about who the shoes were for.

"Emeralds! What would you want with emeralds?" asked 'Ol Mombi.

Ugu hesitated for a moment. He too recalled Dorothy's special request.

"I've been asked to make a fine pair of shoes," he replied.

There was a flit of apprehension among the three visitors at the mention of emeralds and shoes when Blinkie recalled her talk with the two young people on the road to Herku.

"You're making them for Ozma, aren't you?" she

cried out.

Ugu's reaction confirmed the old woman's suggestion.

"Ozma! Ozma?!" cried O'l Mombi. She remembered well long ago how the young Ozma was given to her as a baby by the Wizard of Oz.

Princess Ozma was the adopted daughter of King Pastoria, Ruler of Oz before the time of the Wizard of Oz. It had been 'Ol Mombi who had removed the king from power long ago when her powers were great and her ambition ever greater, though it was the Wizard of Oz who eventually ruled Oz following her defeat by Glinda, thus thwarting 'Ol Mombi's schemes.

'Ol Mombi recalled well how she had transformed the young Ozma into Tip, a young boy who was bound to the old woman by oath and loyalty and did her bidding.

The Emerald Slippers of Oz

Other memories ran quickly through the mind of 'Ol Mombi as she looked over at Dr. Pipt. There was the Powder of Life, which she had obtained from the Crooked Magician, a.k.a.; Dr. Pipt and which she had then made Jack Pumpkinhead come alive.

At the same time, Dr. Pipt recalled well his Powder

of Life; of how Scraps, the Patchwork Girl had been brought to life to serve his beloved wife, Margolotte, only to find that she was much too smart and independent to be anyone's servant.

It had been Scraps who had spilled the Powder of Life onto an old phonograph, rendering it alive; and had also caused his beloved wife, Margolotte, to become petrified after encountering a vial of the Liquid of Petrifaction.

Fortunately, Margolotte eventually regained her former self, in part due to the help of Scraps, a young boy named Ojo and a glass cat named Bungle.

He remembered well just how much trouble the Powder of Life had caused him… and yet, he too felt the pang of desire to do magic returning once again to his inner thoughts.

"Yes… Dorothy wants a pair of shoes made for Princess Ozma for her birthday," Blinkie said solemnly.

Now, the truth was known to everyone inside the old shop, though only Pacifico did not understand its true meaning. His only concern was that Princess Ozma might find out about the new shoes before Dorothy could give them to her.

"Oh she does, does she now?" 'Ol Mombi snapped, thinking of the little girl from Kansas.

All four of the former conjurers of magic stood there, silent in their thoughts and memories of past glory and power. Each relived fond memories from long ago while Pacifico started a fire in the kitchen hearth.

175

The Emerald Slippers of Oz

During this time, Blinkie began to notice a certain reluctance in the eyes of Ugu the Shoemaker; as though the return of his apprentice had dulled his appetite for conjuring magic once more.

As for the other former witch in the shop, she paid little attention to the intentions of Ugu, being far too consumed with thoughts of her own return to power and magical glory.

Even Dr. Pipt failed to notice what Blinkie had seen. His thoughts were divided between reviving Margolotte and regaining his magic powers and so the former Crooked Magician thought of nothing else.

"Why don't I make us some Peppermint and Chamomile tea?" the old woman croaked. There was a general murmur of agreement from the room and Pacifico, who had just returned from the kitchen hearth, escorted Blinkie back to the fire where the old woman proceeded to fill the teakettle from a nearby basin of water.

"Here we go," she declared, picking out a number of Peppermint leaves from her little black satchel. "These will do just nicely!"

Pacifico watched as Blinkie dropped the leaves into the near-boiling water, then replaced the lid on the teakettle and returned it to the heat of the flames.

Blinkie now began to ponder how she might distract the young man while she put her plan into action.

"Please be a dear and fetch me my other satchel there on the workbench in the other room," she asked the bare-footed young man. Her voice was calm and soothing,

176

despite her less than soothing appearance.

Pacifico nodded and made for the main room where the others were gathered. As he vanished past the open doorway, Blinkie reached down into the small pouch within the little black satchel and withdrew the 6-leaf clover that had been so cleverly hidden there days before.

"Let's see what this will do for our reluctant shoemaker," she thought to herself as the teakettle now whistled loudly.

Just then, Pacifico returned with her other black satchel and handed it to the old woman.

Blinkie rummaged through the contents and brought out a single leaf of Chamomile, all the while concealing the 6-leaf clover and smiling and being overly-pleasant.

"Where do you keep your tea cups?" she asked Pacifico.

The young apprentice shuffled through the cupboards nearby and found Ugu's favorite cup, made from leather and standing but a few inches high.

"I think we have a few other cups around here somewhere," said an exasperated Pacifico as he searched through more cupboards and drawers and such.

In time, the young man found several more cups made of fine china and his own pewter teacup.

The Emerald Slippers of Oz

Blinkie poured the Peppermint tea into each of the cups, now arranged on a wooden platter. She then dipped the Chamomile leaf into each cup briefly, commenting to Pacifico that "this will help us sleep better tonight."

"Ow!" cried out Blinkie, pretending she had dipped a finger into the boiling-hot tea of the second-to-last cup.

Pacifico jumped at the sound and offered to help.

"No thank you," replied Blinkie. "I'll be fine." She transferred the Chamomile leaf to her other hand, which just happened to be concealing the 6-leaf clover.

The Emerald Slippers of Oz

Dipping the Chamomile leaf and the concealed 6-leaf clover into the tea contained in the leather cup of Ugu the Shoemaker, Blinkie then placed both back into the small pouch within her little black satchel.

A thin layer of gossamer green mist soon hovered slightly above the tea in the leather cup, which Blinkie gently blew away before the young, bare-footed apprentice could notice.

Meanwhile, 'Ol Mombi and Dr. Pipt watched as Ugu the Shoemaker sat down on his three-legged work stool and examined the two rectangular-shaped emeralds that Pacifico had given him. He was mesmerized by the brilliance of the emeralds and very pleased to note that they were identical in every way.

"These will make my fine shoes even better!" he declared, measuring them with a small wooden ruler.

'Ol Mombi and Dr. Pipt looked at each other warily. Each pondered as to how these shoes of emeralds could be used to their own advantage.

Just then, they heard the old woman in the kitchen shout out in pain.

"Everything all right in there?" asked Ugu, looking up from his workbench and the perfect emeralds sitting there.

A few minutes later, Blinkie and Pacifico returned with a full tray of steaming-hot teacups. Pacifico had even managed to find a small cache of thin biscuits, which were now arranged around the teacups and each looked very inviting.

179

The Emerald Slippers of Oz

"I just burnt my finger a bit making us some Peppermint tea with just a hint of Chamomile," Blinkie confessed. She avoided looking at 'Ol Mombi and Dr. Pipt, both of whom were now eyeing her with mild suspicion.

Blinkie, Pacifico and Ugu each took a cup of Peppermint and Chamomile tea, along with a biscuit while 'Ol Mombi and Dr. Pipt looked on, certain that something was amiss.

When no harm seemed to befall the three tea drinkers, the other two gathered up a cup and a biscuit and enjoyed themselves.

Chapter 30
Dorothy's Audience
With The Queen

D orothy looked back over her shoulder at the receding skyline of Emerald City. It had taken her several hours to get this far, though not so much because of distance than of the local populace, each one stopping to greet her and speak of this and that… and even some of the other.

Dorothy Gale of Kansas, now Princess Dorothy by proclamation of Her Majesty; Princess Ozma, was much beloved by nearly everyone in Oz, though there were a few witches and magicians who held no fondness for the little farm girl from the Great Outside. Her gentle nature and calm assurance allowed her to endure the adulation of the masses, which at times could be quite time consuming.

She was heading south on foot and making good time now. Dorothy knew that when the tallest spires of Emerald City were no longer visible, then the fields where Her Majesty; Queen of the Field Mice lived and ruled.

There was the occasional stop for refreshment along a gently flowing stream here and there, or one of several houses along the way south that served as local

181

inns where people gathered to socialize and do commerce.

Here too, people flocked about Dorothy, asking this and that, and what the other was doing here and there. Gossip was always popular in the Land of Oz.

Now, it was noon and the tallest spire, which so happened to be the personal spire of Princess Ozma within Her mighty palace, was nowhere to be seen from the well-worn brick pathway leading south to the Munchkin River and Quadling Country.

Dorothy turned east towards Munchkin Country and headed across the immense field of clover towards the prairie grasses she knew to be an hour's walk away.

The sun, now an hour or so past the noon hour and Dorothy stood ankle deep in prairie grasses and little scurrying rodents.

Before her stood a small hillock, rising about three feet or so above the flat prairie field, and having the grasses trampled down in such a way as to render the hillock smooth and most distinct from the surrounding countryside.

Dorothy had arrived at the home of the Queen of the Field Mice and she was glad to be there as she looked around for the only mouse wearing a crown, a cape and carrying a small scepter.

There were hundreds and hundreds of mice, scampering about and making a very pleasant sort of chatter as they talked among each other, waiting for the arrival of their monarch.

Dorothy could tell something was afoot when all of

a sudden, every mouse went suddenly silent. Only the sound of the gentle wind against the prairie grasses could be heard. She knew that royalty was approaching.

"Ah, my dear! What a pleasure to see you! Why it's been ages since your last visit," declared the petite rodent that approached from a small opening dug out near the top of the smooth grassy hillock.

She was, of course, wearing a very dainty crown of finely woven gold wire, inlayed with red velvet and very small diamonds, although for the Queen of the Field Mice, they were the perfect size.

She now wore a lovely red velvet cape, which was quite long and two attendant mice wearing snappy little feathered caps held each far corner, never allowing the cape to touch the soil.

The small scepter She bore was *"no larger than a wooden toothpick,"* or so Dorothy always thought.

"Your Majesty..." Dorothy said proudly, bowing her head slightly to her very good friend.

Both Queen and Princess broke out in giggled laughter at their silly behavior. There was a faint roar of approval from the assembled

"What brings you to My humble kingdom, Dorothy?" the Queen inquired. She looked about, hoping not to see Dorothy's usual companion bouncing about, looking for mice to chase.

Dorothy could see that the Queen was a bit nervous and she knew why.

"Toto's not with me today," she assured the royal

rodent, who was visibly relieved. There was a general murmur of relief among the populace as well.

Toto had never hurt a single mouse in all his years in Oz, but his canine instincts were to chase rodents and he just couldn't help himself sometimes.

Fortunately, Toto was still up north in Gillikin Country, visiting the Cowardly Lion, who has recently celebrated his birthday.

"I've had a very odd dream and I think your subjects were in it," she continued on.

Dorothy described the dream in great detail. The little rodent listened with rapt attention, especially when Dorothy mentioned the two large green eyes.

"They had an odd shape to them... not round... more like squares, or rectangles," she said as the Queen of the Field Mice nodded Her head.

The royal rodent also knew about the power and meaning of dreams and recognized the green eyes as soon as She heard Dorothy describe them.

"I believe you were dreaming about the Gemini Emeralds," the Queen suggested.

Dorothy gasped, recalling how long ago, the Queen of the Field Mice and Her subjects had saved the Cowardly Lion from the treacherous odor of the Poppies. She had given the Gemini Emeralds to her friend, the Queen of the Field Mice once she had been declared a Princess of Oz.

Dorothy had never forgotten the Queen's kindness and resourcefulness and the Gemini Emeralds were her way of honoring the Queen and Her subjects.

The Emerald Slippers of Oz

The Queen explained all about Pacifico, his mission, which the Queen confessed She didn't "know who the shoes were for."

Dorothy visited for another hour or so, then considered how she might best be on her way.

"With your permission, I'll be on my way to Herku, where I'm certain I'll find Pacifico and Ugu," Dorothy said quite regally as she bowed deeply.

Once again, both Queen and Princess giggled loudly and for several minutes at their silly behavior. The protocols of royalty seemed lost on the two good friends as they bid each other farewell.

At long last, Dorothy was back among the clover and looking for the brick road that lead south. Not far from where she had turned eastward several hours before, Dorothy knew that the road leading westward towards Lake Quad and on to Winkie Country branched off of the southern route. She was eager to find Pacifico and Ugu the Shoemaker.

Chapter 31
Ugu's Dream

As the Peppermint and Chamomile tea began to soothe Ugu's jittery nerves, he began to nod off, drifting slowly into a dream-like state of mind.

"Magic, magic, magic..." The sound of that word was the sweetest sound running through his mind.

"Magic... What could be better than magic?" His inner mind ran the question back and forth within his dream-like trance. *"And power!"* The idea of magic and power sounded wonderful to Ugu.

But then, the thought of Dr. Pipt, 'Ol Mombi and Blinkie slowly invaded his inner trance, like so much fog rolling into a lush green valley.

"They will be a problem," his dream echoed.

Just then, a momentary spark of truth hovered above the rolling mist of his thoughts and dreams.

"Magic might be the bigger problem," his mind pondered within the vision, *"or would two old witches and a wicked old sorcerer be worse?"*

The essence of the 6-leaf clover now overwhelmed his better judgment as visions of magic and power consumed the old shoemaker.

186

The Emerald Slippers of Oz

Even though Ugu enjoyed making shoes that made people happy, he now convinced his inner thoughts that regaining his old ways of magic would be his greatest joy yet.

"*Yes...*" he thought to himself within the vision. "*In my younger days, I knew quite a lot of magic.*" All memories of Dorothy and Princess Ozma and even his time as a grey dove vanished from thought.

"*I wonder...*" He thought about the shoes which he had been asked to make as a birthday present for the Ruler of Oz. "*What would happen if I could endow them with special powers?*"

No, he couldn't do that. Not for Princess Ozma. No, Dorothy would be furious at him.

"*But those emeralds...*" Once more, the essence of the 6-leaf clover overwhelmed his better judgment and clouded all reason from his inner mind. "*They must be magical in and of themselves.*"

He could tell when he had examined them. Their shape, their bright green color, even the feel of the smooth edges told him these were no ordinary emeralds.

Now, the emeralds floated about his inner mind, taunting his thoughts and consuming his will to resist.

Ugu suddenly awoke with a start. The little shop was growing slowly darker as evening twilight had begun.

Nearby, Pacifico was setting up their cots, which the old shoemaker and his apprentice used for sleep. The three visitors were nowhere to be seen.

"Our guests are staying at the inn next door," he

explained to Ugu, who was still somewhat flustered by the vision of the emeralds. "They said they would return in the morning."

After a light meal, both men settled down for the night and Ugu returned to his dreams of magic and power and glory.

Chapter 32
The Emerald Slippers

U gu woke up the next morning in a fog. *"It must have been the tea that Blinkie made,"* Ugu thought. "I wonder if she put something in it," he mumbled to himself.

"Did you say something?" Pacifico asked.

"No, I was just thinking to myself. I feel out of sorts today," Ugu replied.

"I feel just fine. Must be something in the weather," Pacifico said cheerfully.

"Perhaps..." Ugu muttered absently. He headed for the back room where the kitchen hearth was and got the old metal tea kettle that Blinkie had made tea in the night before. The old cobbler looked in it and even smelled it to see if he could detect any odor or unusual residue in it. He couldn't find a thing wrong with the old pot, so he washed it out and felt better about it.

In the back of his mind though, an odd tingling sensation hovered just below his awareness.

Ugu began his usual morning routine, preparing his workbench for the upcoming day's work while Pacifico prepared some hot oatmeal and honey, along with fresh apple juice. This was Ugu's favorite morning meal and the

189

old cobbler's apprentice wanted to improve Ugu's rough start.

Following Pacifico's excellent breakfast, Ugu felt much better and set about the task at hand.

"I need some of that green velvet material up in the cabinet, Pacifico, if you would please," Ugu requested, "and maybe some of that silver ribbon might look good along the edges?"

"Silver?" Pacifico asked doubtfully.

"Yea, I think silver might just be the thing to make them sparkle," the old cobbler replied.

Pacifico rummaged about in the cabinets for Ugu's needs and found the green velvet and silver ribbon in no time.

"We're out of those nice bronze tacks I like to use for special occasions," Ugu said with some disappointment. "Could you run down to the smithey's shop and pick up a bushel? And while you out, I saw some very nice green tassels in that dress shop by the mayor's house that I can use as well."

Pacifico nodded and headed out the door as Blinkie, Dr. Pipt and 'Ol Mombi were just walking in.

For the next hour or so, Ugu set about prepping his finest leather for the cutting wheel as his three guests watched with rapt attention.

When Pacifico returned with the tacks and tassels, Ugu had completed the cutting of the leather and had both shoe forms draped with the highly polished and oiled leather.

The Emerald Slippers of Oz

While the old cobbler pursued his trade, 'Ol Mombi sat silently, wondering if the large emeralds they had seen the day before might be magical in nature. Emeralds of that size often were and these were the biggest she had ever seen.

As the old witch pondered the nature of magical emeralds, Blinkie and Dr. Pipt discussed the smell of the leather, though each also harbored thoughts about the nature of the large emeralds from the night before.

"Pacifico, would you take those walking boots and deliver them to the Orchard Keeper?" Ugu asked his apprentice as he pointed to a very nice pair of plain leather boots he had completed the day before. "Be sure to stop by the thread shop and pick up some gold thread on your way back. I want to do some nice embroidery work on these slippers."

As Pacifico headed out the door, the odd sensation Ugu had felt earlier that morning returned, though still only vaguely.

By noontime, Ugu had completed the shaping of the leather into something resembling a pair of slippers, though they clearly had a way to go before completion.

Pacifico had yet to return from his errand, so 'Ol Mombi offered to prepare lunch for the cobbler's shop.

"I make a fine stew," she boasted.

Since Ugu, Blinkie and Dr. Pipt hadn't eaten since morning, they eagerly agreed.

'Ol Mombi had no trouble finding some fresh carrots, potatoes, celery, mushrooms and even a fibrous

191

tuber that resembled meat in both appearance and flavor, among the cabinets of the back room.

Not long after, the large iron pot hanging above the crackling fire in the hearth steamed happily with a brown, bubbly stew.

The smell was quite savory, though the old sorceress was not quite satisfied.

"I couldn't find any pepper!" she complained, "and your apprentice isn't here to get some."

"I have some in my satchel," Blinkie suggested, fumbling through the little black satchel and producing the little Pepperspice box she had brought with her from home.

"Ol Mombi accepted it, though somewhat reluctantly as she was still suspicious of the *old hag from Jinxland.*"

Returning to the kitchen hearth, 'Ol Mombi made to season the stew when she examined the little Pepperspice box carefully. Something about it looked oddly familiar, though the old woman couldn't quite put her withered finger on it.

Nonetheless, she added the Pepperspice to the stew and after a few minutes of simmering, served up a delicious stew that all four agreed was the best stew each had eaten in many years.

After lunch, Ugu sat at his workbench and pondered how he might proceed with the slippers he was making for Princess Ozma.

Slowly, he felt that odd, nagging sensation

returning once again, though once more, it lurked just below his awareness.

Even though 'Ol Mombi had made the stew, he couldn't help but wonder if the two old witches were working together on some magic against him... or maybe it had something to do with the shoes. And what of Dr. Pipt? Could he be in on it too?

"*No,*" Ugu thought. He was certain Dr. Pipt didn't have anything to do with the tea or the stew.

Even though he felt quite odd, Ugu continued working on the slippers as he fastened the green velvet material over the leather. The bronze tacks worked nicely holding the material in place.

He aimlessly thought of magic again. Ugu still thought about the time he had been a grey dove and he decided that he didn't want to go back to those days, and the thought that he could once again become a great magician sounded great to the old cobbler.

"The power..." Ugu mumbled quietly.

"Did you say something?" Blinkie asked abruptly.

Ugu had interrupted her own thoughts of wanting to return to Jinxland and rule over the people.

"No, I was just thinking out loud about the design for these slippers. It takes a lot of power to make such a fine pair of slippers for a Princess of Oz," Ugu replied, hoping that his little white lie would satisfy the old woman with the one eye.

"Did you say powder?" Dr. Pipt chimed in. It seems that Ugu had interrupted the old man's train of thought.

"No... No... I was just talking about the shoes and the design," Ugu said in an exasperated tone of voice.

Now the old cobbler was fully frustrated at everyone for making him lose his own train of thought.

Dr. Pipt just shook his head and returned his gaze to the object of everyone desire.

'Ol Mombi looked forward to regaining her magic and the shoes seemed like a great way to do just that.

"Those emeralds just have to have magic in them," she thought. *"And if they don't, I'll just have to find a way to put magic in them."*

The Emerald Slippers of Oz

Dr. Pipt now sat silently, thinking of Margolotte and how wonderful it would be to see her again. He just hoped that he could regain his magical powers so that he might revive her. The old man looked forward to her great cooking. They had been together for such a long time that he sadly missed her. And yet, he also longed to return to his days of magic.

It was quite a conundrum for the former Crooked Magician. Magic and his longing to regain it had caused a lot of heartaches for Dr. Pipt and Margolotte.

Now, he was staring at Ugu as the old cobbler continued hammering tacks into velvet and leather. His thoughts returned to magic and how these shoes might help him in his quest.

Blinkie rummaged through her little black satchel of herbs, flowers and such while she pondered on the thought of how she might regain her own magical powers.

As she did, 'Ol Mombi glanced over at Blinkie and tried to recall where she had seen that old Pepperspice box Blinkie had lent her only an hour before, but it had been years since 'Ol Mombi had practiced her magic and she just couldn't remember.

Maybe she had seen it or one like it somewhere else…

Just then, Pacifico returned from his delivery, bearing the gold thread Ugu had requested. He was relieved that the three guests just ignored him. They had made him very uneasy… very uneasy indeed!

Now, the bare-footed cobbler's apprentice looked

over Ugu's progress and was very pleased. He thought about the possibility of meeting Princess Ozma, something he had never done before, and the thought made him very happy, even more than having met Princess Dorothy the month before.

He had always envisioned the day when he might meet the lovely and benevolent Ruler of Oz.

And now, he had played a part in the making of the slippers, though in reality, he had not actually constructed the shoes. It had been him though, that had been gifted the Gemini Emeralds, which were to be the crowning gems for Her Majesty's birthday present.

"Pacifico, would you hand me that leather punch from the other bench," Ugu requested.

Pacifico's visions of glory quickly left him as he searched for the tool. Despite his uneasiness with the ever-present guests and the occasional needs of Ugu, the bare-footed apprentice with the green toenails and gold ankle chain hadn't even considered that the three former conjurers of magic were now actively engaged in their own devious plots. Not even in a hundred years would that thought have occurred to him.

Of course, in Oz, what's a hundred years?

"Could you sharpen that needle for me while I sketch out a design for the gold thread accents?" Ugu asked as his apprentice handed him the leather punch.

Pacifico nodded and sat down at the far bench and applied the needle to the well-worn honing stone.

Dr. Pipt's thoughts turned to the Powder of Life. It

had been the greatest feat of magic he had ever performed, though it had taken him six years of constant stirring and vigilance to create.

He remembered now that he had put the magical powder in an old pepper spice box that Margolotte had discarded. He wondered if it was the same one that Blinkie had now. The old former magician with the crooked limbs recalled well how 'Ol Mombi had bargained with him for the Powder of Life long ago.

"Yes, she had done her magic... Evil, bad magic at that, during her time," Dr. Pipt thought. *"If I ever regain my old magic, never again will I trust that cunning sorceress... or that old, one-eyed hag either."*

He looked at Ugu, who was now firmly engaged in sewing an ornate pattern of gold thread onto the overlapping green velvet front piece of the slippers.

"I don't believe I'll trust him either," Dr. Pipt thought.

As if Ugu could have read the old magician's mind, Ugu stopped in mid-sew.

"Did you say something, Dr, Pipt?" he asked the old man with the very crooked limbs.

"No...Uh.. No..." he stammered as Ugu looked directly at him.

"I thought I heard you say something," Ugu replied.

"I was just thinking of my wife, Margolotte," Dr. Pipt lied.

There was a moment's hesitation as an uneasy stillness overcame the little shop.

The Emerald Slippers of Oz

"She fine... She's just fine!" 'Ol Mombi snapped.

Pacifico, Blinkie and Ugu all looked at both 'Ol Mombi and Dr. Pipt with surprise and suspicion while they both glared at each other.

Ugu noticed that nagging feeling growing once more and sensed that it was nearly ready to breach the surface of his mind, like a whale coming up for air from the deep waters below.

After a few tense moments, Ugu returned to his labors and within the hour, the gold embroidery work was complete.

"Now for those tassels, Pacifico," Ugu said happily. His work was nearly complete and his pride was most evident, though the apprehension was still nearby.

Once the green tassels were affixed to the front of the slippers, Ugu suggested they take a break for some food and refreshments.

"Pacifico, be a good man and run down to the bakers and grab us a nice blueberry pie," Ugu said cheerfully. "It's been a rough day and I know how much you love blueberry pie."

The old cobbler was quite correct about his young bare-footed apprentice and his love of blueberry pie.

"After all," he continued, "everyone loves pie!"

Pacifico laughed heartedly and headed out the door and down the street towards the bakers shop on the next block.

"Now, as for these emeralds," Ugu said curiously as he held them aloft and studied their shape and color.

The Emerald Slippers of Oz

Both former witches and the former magician leaned forward, eager to see the finely-cut green gems for themselves. Their desire for magic and their belief that these gems held the answer was quite obvious, though Ugu saw only the emeralds at the moment.

"How to attach them..?" Ugu said absent-mindedly, talking more to himself than to anyone in the shop.

With the exception of the addition of the Gemini Emeralds, the slippers were now complete and the old cobbler set the gemstones down onto the front over-lapping green velvet that he had just finished embroidering with the gold thread.

He had thought to try out several positions for the gemstones when suddenly; a bright green flash filled the entire shop, blinding everyone within. The flash was accompanied by a viscous roar of thunder, which knocked everyone off their chairs and flat onto their backs.

For several minutes, the only sound that could be heard within the old cobblers shop was the sharp, rapid breaths of all four people as they struggled to regain their senses.

Chapter 33
The Resurrection of Old Magic

"Hmmm. That not only looks wonderful, it smells even better!" Pacifico declared as he pointed out the still-warm blueberry pie now cooling on the nearby shelf of the Baker's shop.

The Baker smiled and reached out for the moist shell of pastry and blueberries. The bottom was still hot and he had to juggle it between both hands until it became cool enough to carry.

"You plan on eating this all by yourself?" he asked the bare-foot apprentice. Both men laughed heartedly.

"Nope! Ugu sent me over. We have visitors in the shop and he's too busy to come himself," Pacifico explained.

"Well then, here's a slice from another one for the journey back. We wouldn't want you starve on the way home, now would we?" the Baker said jokingly. Once again, both men laughed. He knew how much Ugu's apprentice loved blueberry pie.

The Emerald Slippers of Oz

"Thanks!" Pacifico exclaimed. He headed out the door, a full pie in one hand and a slice in the other. Before he had even made it down the street and around the corner, the slice had vanished, leaving only crumbs in his hand. He wiped his mouth with his sleeve and burped loudly, eliciting some chuckles from a nearby fruit stand.

"Everyone loves pie, don't they Pacifico?" the owner of the fruit stand declared.

Pacifico continued on his way, admiring the remaining pie as he walked confidently along the cobblestones of the streets of Herku. He felt happy, knowing that Ugu was nearing completion of Princess Ozma's birthday present, though the visitors he had mentioned to the Baker still concerned him. Something about them made him uneasy, though he couldn't quite understand why.

As Pacifico rounded the corner and headed down to the cobbler's shop where he and Ugu resided, he felt a sudden wave of fear, followed by a bright flash of green light that seemed to engulf the entire street and the surrounding houses.

Pacifico quickened his pace and in a matter of moments, was inside the shop and staring down at Ugu and the visitors, all four of whom were gasping for breath. He quickly set the blueberry pie down on the work table and helped Ugu to his feet.

"Are you alright? What happened? What was that flash of green light?" he asked in rapid succession. Ugu could not respond at first, but sat down on his stool and caught his breath.

Pacifico helped the other three get up from the floor and sat each one down on the nearby workbench.

After a few minutes, Ugu seemed a bit more composed, though something about his eyes didn't seem quite right to his apprentice.

In fact, Pacifico noticed that all four of them looked somewhat different, though he wasn't sure quite what was different about them. Something in their eyes seemed odd, sort of distant and vague.

Ugu tried to explain what had happened, but he was unsure and he kept mumbling something about old magic and such. His gaze was unfocused and the old cobbler made no sense.

By now, the other three had regained their composure, though Pacifico saw the same look in their eyes that he had seen in Ugu's eyes.

Something was very wrong in the old cobbler's shop.

It was 'Ol Mombi who struck first. She had recognized almost instantly that the green flash was the manifestation of magic bursting forth from the emeralds.

The old sorceress jumped up from the workbench with surprising speed and grabbed the Emerald Slippers before anyone could react. She cast off her old boots in a single motion and quickly put the newly created shoes upon her withered old feet.

"Mine!!!" screamed 'Ol Mombi. She turned to face the rest of the people in the shop and began to recite an old incantation from long ago. The words flowed out like water and the old woman was thrilled that she could finally recall her old magic. Her eyes sparkled with an Evil glint that Blinkie, Dr. Pipt and even Ugu recognized.

'Ol Mombi was now fully engaged in her spell of transformation, which she had aimed directly at the blueberry pie sitting on the nearby table.

"Mutare a pica, uinculis et dominabuntur omnes!" she repeated, over and over as the blueberry pie began to shake and bounce upon the table.

Pacifico and the others were stunned into silence and nearly frozen in place as they watched 'Ol Mombi perform her ancient magic against the pastry.

The old woman had intended to transform the pie into a web of chains and trap everyone else within, but just then, an odd thing happened.

The blueberry pie leaped up into the air, hovered above the work table and spun about rapidly before bursting apart and transforming into a dozen blueberry pies.

'Ol Mombi screamed as the pies settled back down onto the table. It was clear to everyone there that she had failed in her magic and Ugu was about to rush forward and grab the old woman when she screamed in pain.

The old woman reached down and flung the Emerald Slippers from her feet, desperate to be rid of them.

"They're burning me!!!" she screamed in agony as the shoes flew across the floor, landing just in front of

The Emerald Slippers of Oz

Blinkie.

The old woman with one eye quickly reached down and grabbed the Emerald Slippers before Ugu or Pacifico could reach them.

Just like 'Ol Mombi had done moments before, Blinkie flung off her tattered shoes and slipped her wrinkled old feet into the Emerald Slippers. The same Evil glint appeared in her one good eye.

"Mine!!!" she screamed, just as the old sorceress from Gillikin Country had done... and just like 'Ol Mombi, Blinkie began her own incantation of magic which had returned to her memory at the flash of the green light.

The old one-eyed woman reached down into her little black satchel and retrieved the 6-leaf clover. She waved it about as she chanted her spell of ancient magic.

"Omnia pone somnum sempiternum!" Blinkie repeated over and over. The old witch from Jinxland had intended to put everyone else in the old cobbler's shop to sleep forever, but just then, an odd thing happened.

The shop suddenly began filling up with flowers of all varieties and colors. There were roses and geraniums, begonias and tulips, tiger lilies and orange blossoms, until the floor was covered with all manner of flora reaching up to the bottom of the work bench.

Once again, Ugu thought to rush forward and grab the old woman when she screamed in pain.

The old, one-eyed woman reached down and flung the Emerald Slippers from her feet, desperate to be rid of them.

The Emerald Slippers of Oz

"They're burning me!!!" she screamed in agony as the shoes flew across the floor, landing just in front of Dr. Pipt, though he couldn't quite tell where because of the carpet of flowers strewn across the floor.

Dr. Pipt quickly reached down and searched with his hands for the Emerald Slippers among the flowers.

Moments later, the Crooked Magician found the elusive slippers and held them high above his head.

"Mine!!!" he screamed, just as 'Ol Mombi and Blinkie had done before. He thrust his feet into the Emerald Slippers and felt the rush of magic course through his body.

Reaching down into Blinkie's little black satchel, Dr. Pipt retrieved the little Pepperspice box that 'Ol Mombi had used so well. The memory of the little Pepperspice box came flooding across his mind as he scattered the flowers about with his newly-clad feet.

"Now I remember!" he exclaimed. "This had been the box I kept the Powder of Life in when I sold it to you, you old witch!!"

He pointed directly at 'Ol Mombi, who was rubbing her feet and moaning in pain.

"But how did you get it?!" he asked Blinkie.

The one-eyed witch fumbled for an explanation.

"I got it from a merchant selling spices and such long ago!" she cried out. She too was in much pain and could offer no other explanation.

'Ol Mombi thought back to her days when magic came freely to her and the Powder of Life was in her possession. She now recalled having given the little Pepperspice box to a merchant when she had exhausted her supply of the magical powder.

"It matters not now!" declared Dr. Pipt. "For now I can regain my magic and restore my dear wife!" He held the little Pepperspice box aloft and thought of Margolotte.

"Restitue Margolotte ex alto somno!" he whispered softly, hoping against hope that he might succeed where the others had failed.

There was a moments silence as everyone in the shop stared at Dr, Pipt. He had hoped to revive his dear wife, but just then, an odd thing happened.

The little Pepperspice box suddenly transformed into a long brass horn and began playing a lively tune.

Once more, another of the former conjurers of magic screamed in pain.

Dr. Pipt reached down and flung the Emerald Slippers from his feet, desperate to be rid of them.

"They're burning me!!!" he screamed in agony as the shoes flew through the air, landing on the workbench directly in front of Ugu the Shoemaker.

Pacifico looked at Ugu and saw not the eyes of his mentor, but instead, he gazed into the eyes of someone possessed by something Evil.

"No Ugu! No!!!" he screamed, but the old cobbler heard nothing but the sound of his own desires for the old magic of his youth.

"Mine!!!" Ugu shouted. "I made them and I will keep them for myself!" and just as 'Ol Mombi, Blinkie and

Dr. Pipt had done before, Ugu thrust his feet into the Emerald Slippers and felt the rush of magic course through his body.

Chapter 34
The Pumpkin Carriage

The journey eastward from the Kingdom of the Field Mice was both pleasant and uneventful for Dorothy. By day's end, she had reached the town of Quadwest and a lovely inn by the shores of Lake Quad.

After a fine meal and a pleasant evening by the lakeside, Dorothy spent the night in a very comfortable bed provided by the innkeeper. She dreamt of emeralds and woke up the following morning to a wonderful breakfast.

Soon, the little farm girl from Kansas was once more on the smooth cobblestone road leading eastward towards Winkie Country and the town of Herku where she had left Ugu and Pacifico several months before.

Before long, she noticed an odd, yet familiar contraption heading towards her from the east. It appeared to be a very large pumpkin rolling along on a set of large wooden wagon wheels and pulled by a most curious creature.

"Greetings, Miss Dorothy!" shouted the Scarecrow from his seat inside the large Pumpkin Carriage that now came to a halt before her.

The Emerald Slippers of Oz

Dorothy was very pleased to see her very dear and longest friend in Oz, as well as another of her favorite creatures in Oz, the Sawhorse.

The Sawhorse was a creature that had been brought to life by Dr. Pipt's Powder of Life long ago to serve Jack Pumpkinhead, though now it also served the needs of the Scarecrow. It was created from a log that was notched on one end to form a mouth and had knotholes for eyes. Leather cups served as ears and a leafy branch served as a tail. Its legs were short tree branches and on its feet were golden sheaths that served as horseshoes. A set of leather harnesses attached the creature to the pumpkin carriage.

Although the Sawhorse rarely spoke, on this occasion, it spoke to the little farm girl from Kansas.

"Greetings to you, Princess Dorothy," the living log said softly. "What brings you to this part of Oz?"

"Yes, Dorothy, what brings you this way?" the Scarecrow added.

"I'm on my way to Herku," she replied. "What about you?"

"I felt like a ride in the country in order to give my brains room to think," the Scarecrow explained. He smiled broadly and offered a seat in his Pumpkin Carriage and a ride to Herku.

"You don't mind the extra weight, do you?" she asked the Sawhorse, who shook its head.

"I'm honored to pull a princess anywhere in Oz," the creature assured her.

209

She laughed and recalled a time when the Sawhorse had carried far stranger cargo than a little farm girl from Kansas.

Dorothy hopped up into the Pumpkin Carriage and

sat down across from the Scarecrow. Moments later, the carriage jerked forward, turned around, and they were on their way back eastward towards Herku.

As the Sawhorse pulled the Pumpkin Carriage and its occupants towards the old city, Dorothy explained about her request of Ugu and his transformation back into human form. She told the Scarecrow about Pacifico and his desire to become a shoemaker like Ugu.

The Scarecrow laughed as Dorothy described his bare feet and having never worn shoes.

"Now remember, you can't say a word to Princess Ozma," she reminded her good friend.

"With these fine brains, how could I forget?" he replied.

For the next several hours, the journey was pleasant and uneventful. The blue skies above and the passing landscape, which turned from lush green to vibrant yellow as the pumpkin carriage made its way into Winkie Country, made the journey even more enjoyable as the two old friends talked about this and that... and even some of the other.

As the Pumpkin Carriage passed south of the Merry-Go-Round Mountains, the Sawhorse came to a sudden stop at the approach of someone who seemed to be quite agitated.

"Help me, please!" shouted the blond-haired young man with bare feet and green toenails. He was quite agitated and the Scarecrow leaned out to answer him.

"What can we do to help you?" he asked gently.

The Emerald Slippers of Oz

"I'm looking for Princess Dorothy!" the young man shouted. "Something awful has happened and I don't know who else to turn to!"

With that exclamation, Dorothy came bounding out from the Pumpkin Carriage and landed directly in front of Pacifico, who was clearly upset, but also very glad to see her.

"Dorothy!!" he exclaimed. "Ugu has gone mad! Something happened to the slippers and the others tried to steal them!!!"

By now, both Dorothy and the Scarecrow were quite confused by Pacifico's outburst.

For the next hour or so, the young apprentice tried to explain to Dorothy about his search for emeralds, the visitors to the shop, and Ugu's creation of the Emerald Slippers and what had happened when he did.

"Ugu headed west after the others ran away," he explained. "I don't know where the others went, but they were very frightened when they did."

It was all still very confusing and Dorothy was not sure what exactly was going on, but she recognized the names Pacifico had told her. So did the Scarecrow.

"Hop in and we'll make our way back to Herku as fast as possible," the Scarecrow commanded.

Pacifico did as the man of straw had asked and moments later, the Sawhorse was pulling the Pumpkin Carriage as fast as any of the occupants had ever travelled before.

Within the hour, the Pumpkin Carriage passed

212

through the gates of Herku and on towards the shop of
Ugu the Shoemaker.

Chapter 35
The Kudzu Fields

T he old cobbler's shop was in total disarray.
Tools and leather were strewn about all over
the place. The floor was covered in all
manner of flowers. On a nearby workbench sat ten
blueberry pies while a long brass horn sat on a chair,
playing a lively tune. In a far corner were several small
black satchels, which Pacifico recognized immediately.

"Where did you say they went to?" Dorothy asked
Pacifico, who only shook his head.

"They all ran out the front door and into the streets
of the city," he explained. "They were in such a hurry that
they left behind their possessions." He pointed at the black
satchels nearby. "Ugu looked like something I had never
seen before. His eyes…" It was clear that Pacifico was very
upset about his mentor's whereabouts.

The Scarecrow picked up the brass horn and
stuffed some begonias into it, hoping to muffle the sounds
of the song. They were quickly blown out by the pressure
of the music blowing forth from the horn. He sat it back
down on the nearby workbench with the main end of the
horn facing down onto the worn wood. The sound was
somewhat muffled, which was greatly appreciated by both

The Emerald Slippers of Oz

Dorothy and Pacifico.

"You say they all ran away... even Ugu?" Dorothy pressed the shoemaker's apprentice for an answer. She felt some measure of responsibility for the situation now surrounding her, though the Scarecrow and Pacifico had tried to assure her that she was not responsible for what had happened.

"If I hadn't asked Ugu to make those shoes, none of this would have happened," she said despairingly. Nothing either the Scarecrow or Pacifico said helped matters much, though each tried his best to comfort the little girl from Kansas.

"Where could they have ran off to?" the Scarecrow asked. His brains pulsated within the old burlap sack that was his head. He thought for some time and finally settled on an idea of where he thought Ugu might have gone.

"I'm certain he probably went back to the one place he felt most comfortable at," the Scarecrow suggested.

"The Wicker Palace..." Dorothy whispered.

The Scarecrow nodded in agreement.

"That's where I found him before and I know that's where he's at now," she said assuredly.

"What about the other three?" Pacifico inquired.

Once more, the Scarecrow thought hard and rubbed his head vigorously, hoping to arouse an idea or two. In time, he seemed to come up with an idea or two that might be of use.

"Dorothy, you should go to the Wicker Palace and find Ugu. Reason with him if you can... and argue with him if you can't," the Scarecrow suggested.

Dorothy agreed, then looked at both her old friend, the Scarecrow, and her new friend, Pacifico.

"And what about you two? Will you look for the others?" she said, almost pleading with them.

"Of course," the Scarecrow assured her. Even Pacifico nodded in agreement. He wanted desperately to do something to help Dorothy, who he had come to admire and respect.

With that, the three of them headed back out the front door of the old cobbler's shop and looked up and down the street.

"Dorothy, you take my carriage and head west for the Wicker Palace while Pacifico and I head east for the Great Orchard. I have an idea they may be heading there to hide among the trees," the Scarecrow said confidently.

Moments later, the Pumpkin Carriage was carrying Dorothy out the large bronze gates of the city and westward towards the Wicker Palace.

Pacifico turned to the Scarecrow and looked at the man of straw with much puzzlement.

"Do you really think they are hiding among the trees?" he asked the Scarecrow.

"That's where I would hide if I were them," he replied.

In no time, the Scarecrow and Pacifico were also heading out past the large bronze gates and westward towards the Great Orchard that lay west of the city of Herku.

The Emerald Slippers of Oz

No sooner had they put the city behind them when a large circus wagon, festooned with bunting and painted in vibrant colors came rolling down the cobblestone path from the west.

Pacifico noticed that there appeared to be no animal pulling the wagon, yet it moved along at a very good pace. He watched as it came to a halt just in front of them.

"Greetings, my magnanimous and highly intelligent friend!" declared the Wizard of Oz as he parted the curtains, revealing himself from within the large circus wagon. He was an elderly man with a kind face and very little hair that came to little peaks just above and in front of his ears. He was well-dressed in a velvet waistcoat and pinstriped vest and wearing a dark green top hat.

The Scarecrow returned the greetings and helped the old man down from the wagon.

"And who might this fine young fellow with the lovely green toenails be?" he asked the Scarecrow.

By now, Pacifico was completely stunned by the situation he now found himself facing. In the last few days, he had visited Emerald City, met a rodent Queen who presented him with a pair of stunning emeralds, watched magic being performed and now was face-to-face with two former Rulers of Oz. It was almost more than the young cobbler's apprentice could stand.

The Emerald Slippers of Oz

The Scarecrow introduced Pacifico to the Wizard of Oz, who then proceeded to explain to the old man the circumstances that had brought them together.

"So as I understand it, Ugu, Blinkie, Dr. Pipt and 'Ol Mombi have tried to regain their old magic?" the Wizard said calmly. "And with results not quite up to their expectations?"

The Emerald Slippers of Oz

Pacifico nodded in agreement.

"That explains why my crystal ball went all green and cloudy," he mused. "And now you say that several of them may have escaped into the Great Orchard?"

The Scarecrow shook his head vigorously, causing several strands of straw to float gently down from the burlap sack that was his head.

"Then we're off to see the witches and wizard," the old man chuckled. He leaped back up into the old circus wagon and invited the Scarecrow and Pacifico to join him.

In no time, the old circus wagon lurched forward and the three of them were headed eastward towards the Great Orchard that lay to the east of the Merry-Go-Round Mountains.

"Nice color on them toenails, my boy!" declared the old man, pointing down at Pacifico's feet.

Pacifico blushed with embarrassment.

"But they definitely need some sprucing up!" the old man declared. He reached into a large black leather case underneath his seat and produced a small paintbrush.

Waving it aloft, the old man muttered some words and pointed it at Pacifico's feet.

Pacifico felt a warmth flow over his toes and in a matter of moments, his toenails sparkled just like they had when he had been in Emerald City.

"That's better!" exclaimed the Wizard of Oz.

Just then, a large field of vegetation appeared to one side of the cobblestone road that the old circus wagon and in occupants were traveling on.

To the north of the field of vegetation, they could see the Great Orchard with its many fruit trees.

"What is this place?" asked Pacifico, who had not been this way before.

"This, my boy, is the Kudzu Fields," the old man said proudly.

Pacifico looked very puzzled, as did the Scarecrow.

"What is Kudzu?" the bare-footed apprentice asked the old man.

The Wizard of Oz chuckled softly at the young man's question.

"Pueraria lobata, my dear boy… or, in the vernacular of the peasantry, Kudzu!" the Wizard of Oz declared. "It's a vine, a weed, a clinging, annoying thing to those who don't appreciate its beauty."

Pacifico wrinkled his nose at the odd description, then noticed something unusual in the distance.

Huddled at the edge of the field were two small figures, which Pacifico recognized almost immediately.

"That's them!" he declared, pointing at Dr. Pipt and Blinkie, both of whom seemed almost to be swallowed by the immense carpet of weeds that nearly surrounded them.

The old circus wagon came to a sudden halt just in front of the old witch and the former Crooked Magician.

The Scarecrow recognized Blinkie and remembered how he had defeated her long ago.

The Wizard of Oz also recognized the other of the two people among the clinging vines. It was Dr. Pipt and the old man noticed that the former Crooked Magician appeared just as he had long ago when he was still a Crooked Magician. His limbs were just as crooked and askew as they had ever been.

Blinkie and Dr. Pipt also recognized the occupants of the old circus wagon as well and the fear on their faces was unmistakable.

"Not you!" Blinkie screamed in horror. Her worst fear was now looking directly at her. She recalled well her defeat at the hands of the Scarecrow and now she faced him once again.

The Emerald Slippers of Oz

Her fear now overwhelmed her senses and the old witch with the one eye fled headlong into the Kudzu Fields, oblivious to the clinging, coiling vines that reached out to clutch at the old woman.

Dr. Pipt followed Blinkie into the Kudzu Fields, but unlike the old woman, he found his way through the weeds quite easily, almost effortlessly.

It must have been his crooked limbs that allowed him to navigate the clinging, coiling vines; for Dr. Pipt flowed through the vegetation nearly untouched. His arms and legs carried his crooked body through the dense overgrowth as though they weren't even there.

In no time at all, he had passed through the Kudzu Fields and on into the Great Orchard beyond.

Blinkie however, barely made it into the immense fields when the Kudzu vines found their way around the old woman's arms and legs, capturing her much like a snare would trap an animal in the woods.

In no more than a heartbeat, she was stopped cold in her tracks, held captive by the clinging vegetation now wrapped tightly around her limbs. It seems that with only one good eye, she had been unable to see every vine coming at her from every direction.

The Scarecrow jumped down from the old circus wagon and approached the old woman. He could see the fear in her eyes, but for him, he felt no anger towards the former he had had once defeated long ago.

"I've been told you've been up to no good, Blinkie," he said quite calmly.

222

Blinkie however, was anything but calm. She struggled against the vines that held her tight.

"I think it's time for you to face the music, old woman," the Scarecrow informed her.

No sooner had the man of straw made his declaration when an odd sound came floating eerily over the vast field of Kudzu vines.

It was a strange sound which reminded the Wizard of Oz of something like a cross between a wailing cat caught in a washing machine and a moaning cow.

Chapter 36
Ugu The Grey Dove

The Sawhorse made good time as it pulled the Pumpkin Carriage through the long, winding valley that lead towards the Wicker Palace of Ugu the Shoemaker.

Dorothy worried about Ugu as the carriage lumbered across the cobblestones and was relieved when it came to a stop in front of the gates of the palace.

She got out and assured the Sawhorse that she would be fine.

"Wait here for me. I shouldn't be long," she told the animated log.

Dorothy climbed the many staircases and made her way up the high tower to where she thought Ugu might be.

Sure enough; there, sitting within the large bird nest, was Ugu the Shoemaker. He still had the Emerald Slippers on his feet and Dorothy could tell that he was not quite himself.

"Get back, Dorothy! You can't have them! They're mine!!" he exclaimed, catching Dorothy by surprise. "I made them and I gonna get my magic back!"

Dorothy didn't know quite what to do. She felt

224

even more responsible now for Ugu's dilemma that when she had talked to Pacifico.

"There was something in that tea… and in that stew! I just know it! I can feel the magic racing through my blood!" he cried out. His eyes were filled with madness as he looked at Dorothy.

She could see it too and a great sadness ran through her.

"Oh Ugu, if only I hadn't asked you to make those slippers, then perhaps all of this might not have happened," she said sadly.

She started towards the old shoemaker, hoping to comfort him. Instead, he backed up, fearful that she might

225

try to steal his Emerald Slippers.

Suddenly, a thought crossed the mind of the old shoemaker and he raised his arms above his head.

"Dorothy in aquilam mutare!" he shouted. Ugu had intended to change Dorothy into an eagle, but just then, an odd thing happened.

Ugu began sprouting feathers and a beak and in no time, he had transformed into a large, grey dove. The Emerald Slippers, which had been on his feet, now slipped off his talons and tumbled down onto the floor in front of the large bird nest.

Dorothy stood there, stunned by Ugu's sudden attempt at magic. She cried softly when she saw what he had become and her tears fell upon the floor and onto the Emerald Slippers.

"Oh Ugu, what have you done..." she cried softly.

The large, grey dove flapped his wings repeatedly and cooed loudly. He felt suddenly happy again, the desire for magic now gone from his mind, replaced by the joys he had felt when he had once been a bird.

"Now, now Dorothy. No need to be sad," the grey dove replied. "It's better this way, don't you see?"

Dorothy shook her head and cried some more.

"Dorothy, I truly enjoyed making shoes, but I was also very happy as a bird, even if I was a bit lonely," he explained. "The desire for magic was too much for me and it made me miserable."

Dorothy ceased her tears and looked at Ugu the Grey Dove.

226

The Emerald Slippers of Oz

"Now I can fly once more and look down from the heavens above as I soar among the clouds," he continued.

Dorothy began to understand, but she still felt sad and somewhat responsible for all of Ugu's misadventures.

"Take the Emerald Slippers and return to Emerald City. Give them to Princess Ozma and fulfill my last act as a cobbler. Nothing would make me happier, Dorothy," Ugu the Grey Dove requested.

Dorothy agreed and took the Emerald Slippers with her as she descended the spiral staircases and made her way out to the Pumpkin Carriage.

"Take me home, Sawhorse," Dorothy asked the living log, who nodded politely.

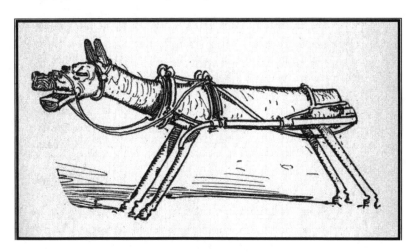

As the Pumpkin Carriage turned for Emerald City and home, Dorothy looked up to see Ugu the Grey Dove flying high above her, circling round and round, occasionally diving down and flying circles around the Pumpkin Carriage.

She smiled as she held the Emerald Slippers close to her and wondered how Pacifico and the Wizard were doing.

Chapter 37
Glinda; Good Witch Of The South

"What is that awful sound?" Pacifico asked. "It seems to be coming from over there." He pointed towards the Great Orchard which lay beyond the Kudzu Fields.

The old man beside him cocked his ear in the direction of the Great Orchard and screwed up his face.

"That is indeed an awful sound, though I do believe I've heard it before, although not since I came to Oz," he said thoughtfully.

Blinkie screamed in horror at the strange sound that was now quite evident among the cling vines and noxious weeds.

"Please!!! Don't make me listen to that awful music!" she cried out, pleading with her captors.

The Scarecrow thought about Blinkie's plea for a few moments as the strange sounds assaulted their senses. He rubbed his head once again, hoping to arouse a solution to the situation at hand.

After a moment or two, the Scarecrow had an idea

229

and addressed the old woman directly.

"I'll spare you the agony of that distressing sound, but only if you agree to answer to Princess Ozma for your wanton acts of magic," he said in an authoritative voice.

Blinkie didn't think twice about the Scarecrow's demands.

"Anything! Anything you say, just take me away from that awful music!" she pleaded despairingly.

With that, the Wizard of Oz reached down into his black bag and produced a small, curved blade on a wooden handle and tossed it to the Scarecrow, who proceeded to cut the old woman free of the captive vines.

Blinkie was clearly grateful at being freed from the Kudzu and became very humbled and quiet.

"Where's the other old woman who was with you in the shop?" the Scarecrow asked her.

Blinkie meekly pointed northward and explained that 'Ol Mombi had fled in that direction when they had left Herku.

"She said something about going home," Blinkie said quietly.

The Wizard of Oz looked over at the Great Orchard and nodded his head.

"Looks like we'll need some help from an old friend of mine," he said calmly. He reached down into a small pocket inside his waistcoat and produced a small silver ring, about the size of small orange. The old man balanced it upright upon his outstretched hand and spun it rapidly, causing the ring to form what looked like a bubble… or so Pacifico thought to himself.

A few minutes later, the three of them watched as a small object approached from the south, floating high above the yellow landscape. As it grew nearer and larger, Pacifico could see that it was a bubble and before long, the bubble began descending from the sky and came to rest just in front of the old circus wagon.

Pacifico watched as the large bubble popped gently, revealing a reclining young lady of immense beauty.

As she rose, the young apprentice saw stunning blue eyes and long hair that flowed down upon her shoulders in stunning, reddish-gold ringlets. She wore a gown of red satin, dotted with rubies of various sizes and shapes. She appeared no older than the young girl he had met along the lakeside during his journey to Emerald City, but even Pacifico could tell by her demeanor that she was much older than even the old man standing beside him.

"Glinda!" exclaimed the Wizard of Oz. "How kind of you to come to our aid."

The Scarecrow was equally pleased to see the Good Witch of the South, who he had known all his life.

"What is that horrid noise coming from beyond these fields?" she asked the Scarecrow, who shook his head vigorously.

"I haven't the vaguest idea," he replied.

She turned her attention to the young man with the bare feet and the gold ankle chain glinting in the sunlight.

Pacifico bowed deeply and expressed his gratitude at meeting the Ruler of the Quadling Country.

"That's a lovely shade of green you're wearing, dear boy," she complimented the young man.

Pacifico blushed and smiled at Glinda.

Only Blinkie seemed ill-at-ease with the arrival of a fellow witch. She hung her head and refused to look directly at Glinda.

The Wizard of Oz started to explain the situation that had required his calling of her, but Glinda assured him she knew full well the reason for his request.

"The Great Book of Records was very revealing in regards to the attempts at magic by Ugu's visitors," she explained.

Pacifico had heard of the Great Book of Records, which he knew to be a complete record of everything that happened in Oz, no matter how important... or not. His was now quite amazed and stunned at knowing that Glinda had known all along about the madness that had occurred in the old cobbler's shop back in Herku.

"Then perhaps you might be so kind as to deal with 'Ol Mombi while this young lad and I track down Dr. Pipt?" the Wizard of Oz requested.

Glinda nodded gently, then turned her attention to the old woman with the black eye patch.

"And as for you, Blinkie," she said sternly at the old woman. "You will obey the Scarecrow's command and travel to Emerald City to await Princess Ozma's judgment for performing magic illegally."

The old woman was frozen with fear. She had tried and failed to regain her old magic and now, her fate was in the hands of others. She felt miserable and quite alone. She nodded in agreement and stared down at her feet.

Glinda turned her attention from the former witch and addressed the Wizard and Pacifico beside the Kudzu Fields.

"See you in Emerald City," she said in a tone of great authority. She sat back down in the small chair, then snapped her fingers and was immediately enveloped in a large bubble. It rose quickly above the immense field of clinging vines and was soon out of sight and heading north.

"Well, we're off to see the Princess!" declared the Scarecrow, who took Blinkie by the arm and pointed her in the direction of the ancient city. They soon rounded a corner of the cobblestone path, leaving the old man and Pacifico all alone.

Before long, the Scarecrow realized that the old woman was having great difficulty walking.

She explained about the Emerald Slippers and how they had burned her feet.

"Perhaps you should go bare-footed?" he suggested. The old woman snorted in disgust and the Scarecrow realized that she would have a difficult time making it all the way to Emerald City, which was a considerable distance away.

He thought for a while as they walked on, then an idea came to the man of straw as they approached an old farm house.

The Scarecrow whistled loudly and a few minutes later, the skies above were peppered with crows.

One of the crows landed on the Scarecrow's shoulders and the two discussed something which Blinkie could not hear.

Moments later, the crow flew up and conversed with his fellow crows and soon, a half a dozen crows swooped down and plucked the old woman from the ground.

Blinkie screamed but found herself unable to do anything else but enjoy the ride.

"My friends will deliver you to Emerald City in no time at all!" shouted the Scarecrow at the receding old witch. "Princess Ozma will meet you there and I'll be along soon!"

Blinkie looked down at the yellow landscape now some distance below and vowed to herself *"never to do magic again."*

Chapter 38
'Ol Mombi's Turn

Glinda floated high above the Great Orchard, heading north in search of 'Ol Mombi. She wondered to herself why the old witch hadn't learned her lesson from long ago.

To have the great Wizard of Oz summon her to find 'Ol Mombi meant a great deal to the Good Witch of the South.

She recalled well how the old humbug magician had handed over the baby Ozma, adopted daughter of King Pastoria, to 'Ol Mombi long ago when he had hoped to inherit the throne of Oz in place of Princess Ozma.

It wasn't that he was Evil by nature, it was just that, being from the Nebraska and knowing only the life of a circus magician and ventriloquist, he thought only of his own needs. Once he had escaped Oz after growing weary of his life as Oz the Terrible, O.Z. Diggs, as was his true name, returned to his life in the circus in Nebraska, only to return to Oz years later, a changed man.

Now, he was much beloved by all in Oz, including Glinda, Dorothy and Princess Ozma.

'Ol Mombi though, was quite Evil by nature and when O.Z. Diggs had given her the baby Ozma, she had transformed the fairy princess into Tip, a young boy who served her as bonded servant for many years.

It had been Glinda who had forced the old witch to disenchant Tip and return to him to the personage of Princess Ozma, who then forgave 'Ol Mombi and permitted her to live.

At the time, Glinda had forced 'Ol Mombi to drink from the Forbidden Fountain, thus forgetting her Evil past.

Now, 'Ol Mombi, along with Blinkie, Dr. Pipt and even Ugu the Shoemaker had attempted to regain their former magical skills, though by Blinkie's account, they had all failed miserably.

"And to think that she was going to use their magic for Evil by a gift of Emerald Slippers that Dorothy had wanted to give Princess Ozma for Her birthday," Glinda thought to herself as she floated high above the Winkie countryside. *"Yes... 'Ol Mombi must be stopped."*

She was more than happy to help find the old witch and stop her from performing magic in defiance of Princess Ozma's edict against illegal magic.

Glinda looked down at the passing countryside, which spread out as a vast yellow canopy of vegetation, farmlands and small villages. She knew 'Ol Mombi was very crafty and resourceful... but old.

Floating gently in her bubble, seated as she was, Glinda commanded the bubble to head north past the Tin Palace of the Tin Woodman. She was certain 'Ol Mombi would avoid such a place where she might be captured.

Finally, in the late afternoon, Glinda found the old

witch near the Winkie River, cowering beneath a yellow stone bridge that crossed over the slowly flowing waters.

'Ol Mombi looked up in great surprise as Glinda, floating high above her, swooped down and landed upon the yellow stone of the bridge.

Once more, the bubble pooped gently, revealing the Good Witch of the South.

"No more magic for you, old woman!" Glinda declared. She reached down beside the small chair she had been reclining on and drew forth a great magic wand which she waved at the old witch.

Before 'Ol Mombi could utter a sound, she found herself encased in a large bubble of her own and was unable to effect an escape by any means she knew of.

"No!!!" she screamed in terror. She knew instantly that any possibility of escape had vanished, along with her failed attempt at regaining her magic.

Glinda renewed her own bubble and floated up into the skies, followed by 'Ol Mombi's bubble. They headed east towards Emerald City at a very leisurely pace.

"What are you doing?!" 'Ol Mombi screeched. "Where are you taking me? I haven't done anything! I've been minding my own business. I..."

"Be quiet! You know very well what you've been up to. You and Blinkie and Dr. Pipt and even Ugu have been up to no good!" Glinda said angrily.

"I have... not," the old woman stuttered.

"You have attempted to practice Evil magic, as you did long ago," Glinda said more calmly now.

"I..." the old woman started to say.

"Not another word from you!" Glinda commanded. "I'm taking you to Emerald City to face Princess Ozma and await your fate, along with the others."

'Ol Mombi became quite meek and submissive at Glinda's reproach.

"You all knew that magic was forbidden to you... and yet you have all once again attempted to practice it," Glinda announced from her seat within the bubble.

'Ol Mombi attempted to glare at Glinda, but she ignored the old woman as they neared the tall spires and domes of Emerald City.

The old witch thought back to her glory days as a powerful sorceress and soon realized that it wasn't going to be a good day for her... or the others.

Suddenly, old age and despair set in on the old witch.

Chapter 39
Victor Columbia Edison

O nce the Scarecrow and Blinkie had departed, the Wizard of Oz turned his attention to the problem of Dr. Pipt. "We'll have to do something about these Kudzu vines," he said while scratching his head in deep thought. In no time at all, an answer came to the old magician.

Reaching back down into his black leather case, the Wizard of Oz retrieved the small curved blade on a long wooden handle.

"This sickle should do the trick!" he declared. Waving the curved blade before the Kudzu Fields and muttering some magic words, the Wizard of Oz commanded the weeds to part, creating a path that lead directly through them and on into the Great Orchard.

The old circus wagon made good time passing through the cleared path and in no time was weaving its way along the Great Orchard.

"That horrid sound is getting louder," Pacifico observed as the old circus wagon bounced along, weaving

241

back and forth among the fruit trees.

"Indeed it is, my boy," replied the old magician, "and yet, it seems oddly familiar."

Soon, the old circus wagon came to an abrupt halt in front of an old apple tree where Dr. Pipt was trapped high among the branches and a most unusual contraption was stationed at the apple tree' base.

"Make it stop!!!" Dr. Pipt cried out from his perch high among the branches.

Both Pacifico and the Wizard of Oz screwed up their faces at the sound coming forth from the contraption at the base of the tree.

It was a tall, wooden table that had a large golden horn affixed to its center. From the golden horn came a most unusual sound that neither Dr. Pipt nor Pacifico recognized.

"It sounds all tinny and scratchy," Pacifico observed. "Nothing like anything I've ever heard."

The old magician thought for a moment while Dr. Pipt squirmed about on his branch.

"Wasn't this thing once yours?" he asked the crooked man among the apples.

"Yes!" admitted Dr. Pipt. "It was horrid then, but now it's driving me mad!!!" Please!! Make it stop!!!

242

The Emerald Slippers of Oz

The Wizard of Oz chuckled at the turn of events that had trapped the former Crooked Magician in an apple tree. It had been his Powder of Life that had created the living phonograph long ago and now that same creation had returned to its creator.

"Hmmm…" thought the old magician. He pondered the situation as the awful sound coming from the golden horn kept playing on. He then approached the contraption and reached down to lift the lid.

"Pardon me," he said politely as he lifted the lid, revealing the inside of the large wooden table.

Both Dr. Pipt and Pacifico watched as the Wizard of Oz fumbled about with the insides of the contraption and produced what looked like a large sewing needle from within.

"This needle is quite dull, which would explain the

odd sounds coming from this creation," he explained.

Pacifico looked at the dull needle and recognized immediately what needed to be done.

"Ahhh! I know how to solve that problem!" he declared. "Ugu often had me sharpen his needles for sewing leather when they became dull."

Dr. Pipt looked down from his perch as Pacifico searched the ground below.

It took the young cobbler's apprentice a few minutes to locate what he was looking for.

"Here we go!" he declared, picking up the small flint stone that he knew would serve his purpose.

Taking the needle from the Wizard of Oz, Pacifico rubbed it upon the small flint stone for a few minutes. When he had completed his task, he showed it to the old magician, who smiled broadly.

The Wizard of Oz took the now-sharpened needle from Pacifico and replaced it within the large wooden table. He closed the lid and moments later, a most beautiful sound emerged from the large golden horn.

"That's much better!" declared the Wizard of Oz.

Dr. Pipt seemed very pleased that the awful sound that had trapped him within the apple tree had improved, but he soon realized that his troubles had just begun.

"That's lovely music, but what kind of music is it?" Pacifico asked.

"That, my boy, is opera!" he declared. "I used to listen to it during my days with the circus."

The Wizard of Oz listened for a few minutes, then a

smile appeared upon his wrinkled face.

"I do believe this particular number is Ave Maria... One of my favorite songs!" he exclaimed.

The old magician looked up at Dr. Pipt and crooked his finger at him, indicating that the former Crooked Magician should come down from his perch among the apples.

"And now to deal with you!" he declared as Dr. Pipt jumped down from the lower branch he had climbed onto.

As Dr. Pipt stood there, awaiting his fate, Pacifico looked over at the odd wooden contraption that was still playing its music, though now the sound was much more pleasing than it had been.

"Is it alive?" he asked absently mindedly.

No sooner had Pacifico asked his question when the music stopped and the contraption spoke.

"Indeed I am!" it declared. "And my name is Victor Columbia Edison."

The contraption now explained its past and how it had come to the Great Orchard.

"I am a phonograph, brought to Life by Dr. Pipt... But he drove me away because my music did not appeal to him," explained the old phonograph. "I've been playing my music for so long now, but no one wants to listen to me. Everyone runs away at the music I played because my needle was so dull."

Pacifico felt sad, as did the old Wizard of Oz. Even Dr. Pipt felt some pity for the thing he had accidently created so long ago.

"I have wandered these lands for as long as I can remember, hoping to find a place here my music will find loving ears," the old phonograph continued on.

The Wizard of Oz smiled at the odd contraption and at Pacifico.

"I do believe I may have the perfect audience for your lovely music," he assured the old phonograph.

The old magician now returned his attention to Dr. Pipt, who shrank at the sudden attention.

"As for you, Dr. Pipt," he said very sternly," you will return with us to Emerald City to face Princess Ozma's judgment for practicing illicit magic."

With that proclamation, the Wizard of Oz passed his hand before the Crooked Magician and uttered his magic words.

Within moments, Dr. Pipt found his crooked limbs straightened out and returned to his former self. He bowed his head in subservience and agreed to accompany them to Emerald City.

"You too, Vic!" the Wizard of Oz declared.

"Vic?" Pacifico said in a puzzled voice.

"Yes. As I recall, Scraps the Patchwork Girl named it that many years ago," he replied.

"Indeed she did, but I prefer my official name if you please?" the old phonograph asserted.

The Wizard of Oz smiled and clapped his hands.

"So be it, Victor Columbia Edison!" he exclaimed.

After a quick snack of apples and pears from a

nearby pear tree, the Wizard of Oz, Pacifico, Dr. Pipt and Victor Columbia Edison were seated within the old circus wagon and on their way to Emerald City.

Chapter 40
Ozma's Judgment

The Grand Hall where Princess Ozma held court was packed. All manner of citizens of Emerald City, the local populace from the surrounding countryside and many luminaries from all four provinces of Oz were in attendance on this most unusual day.

Standing before the gathered throng was Princess Ozma, resplendent in Her royal gown and wearing the Emerald Slippers which Dorothy had brought back from the Wicker Palace of Ugu the Grey Dove.

Seated in a small chair to the right was Princess Dorothy, who had provided testimony an hour or so before regarding the events of the last few days.

Beside her was Glinda; Good Witch of the South and Ruler of Quadling Country, in the southern region of Oz. She too had provided testimony earlier that day.

To the left of Princess Ozma was the Wizard of Oz, whose testimony they had just heard not moments before.

By his side was Pacifico, who had also provided testimony about his mentor, Ugu and the acts of magic he had seen in the old cobbler's shop.

Despite Dorothy's pleadings, Pacifico stood there,

248

bare-footed and sporting his now customary green coat of
nail polish on his toenails. His gold ankle chain gleamed in
the sunlight that streamed in from the far window.

Standing before Her Royal Highness were the four
former conjurers of magic.

On one end was Blinkie, former Queen of the
witches of Jinxland. Next to her was Dr. Pipt, a citizen of
Munchkin Country and the creator of the Powder of Life.
Beside him was 'Ol Mombi, former sorceress of Gillikin
Country and one-time guardian of the baby Ozma. Finally,
there was Ugu the Shoemaker, who now stood before
Princess Ozma in the form of a grey dove.

There was a hushed anticipation as Princess Ozma
strolled forward to address each of the former witches and
magicians of Oz.

"Each of you has heard testimony from these
esteemed witnesses, as well as visual proof from the Magic
Picture and written proof from the Great Book of Records,
which confirms that you have all attempted to practice
magic in defiance of my Royal Order forbidding the
practice of magic," the Royal Ruler of Oz explained. Her
voice was clear and resounding and no one in the Great
Hall doubted Her regal authority.

"What do you have to say for yourselves?" she
intoned.

The four former conjurers of magic shuffled their
feet and looked down at the green marble stone of the
Great Hall.

None spoke and the Great Hall remained totally

silent.

"Very well!" Princess Ozma exclaimed.

She approached the line of former witches and magicians with great authority and composure.

"For each of you, the waters from the Forbidden Fountain shall be your punishment," proclaimed the Royal Monarch of Oz. She indicated the three persons standing before Her.

"For you, Ugu… You yourself have administered your own punishment," Princess Ozma said more gently to the grey dove standing before Her. "You shall remain a grey dove for the rest of your life, though I suspect you will find this sentence more agreeable than your comrades."

There was a murmur among the throngs of people, animals and creatures gathered within the Great Hall.

Everyone agreed that Princess Ozma had shown great compassion for those who would defy Her rule forbidding the performance of magic.

Only 'Ol Mombi spoke up, looking at her former servant with great disdain.

"They may accept your judgment… but I never will!!!" the old woman shouted. "Someday, I'll return and have my revenge!"

The silence within the green marble hall was overwhelming as Princess Ozma strolled back and forth before the four former conjurers of magic.

"Perhaps, 'Ol Mombi…. but not today," She assured the old former sorceress.

The Emerald Slippers of Oz

The crowd in the Great Hall erupted in shouts of joy and triumph. Once more, Princess Ozma had displayed Her compassion and good will against the face of Evil.

Moments later, several guards brought forth thimbles of water from the Forbidden Fountain and compelled each of the three people to drink the waters that would erase their memories of what they had done.

Moments later, all three former witches and magician wore blank faces and equally blank memories.

Just then, Victor Columbia Edison, who had been given a place of honor in the Court of Princess Ozma, began playing a lively rag-time tune that made nearly everyone in the Great Hall cheer and begin dancing happily.

Even the Sawhorse joined in, now wearing a lovely headpiece designed by Princess Ozma Herself, as a gift to the animated log for its role in the grand adventure of the Emerald Slippers.

The Emerald Slippers of Oz

Ugu the Grey Dove thanked Princess Ozma for Her compassion and flew off through a nearby window, heading due east for Herku. He had been spared the memory-erasing waters and was grateful for that.

Princess Ozma noticed that her dear friend, Dorothy Gale, of Kansas was not as happy as everyone else in the Great Hall seemed to be.

She took her dearest friend by the hand and led her to a small antechamber directly behind the Great Hall.

"What is wrong, Dorothy?" She inquired. "You seem troubled by all of this."

Dorothy was indeed troubled by the recent turn of events. She had felt responsible for all that had happened and it showed in her eyes.

The Emerald Slippers of Oz

"If I hadn't asked Ugu to make those slippers for you, none of this would have happened," she said meekly. Slowly, tears began to fall softly upon her cheeks.

Princess Ozma reached into her royal gown and retrieved a small, light green, silken handkerchief and dabbed Dorothy's tears away.

"Dorothy, Dorothy," She said, trying to comfort the crying girl from Kansas. "If you hadn't asked Ugu to make these fine slippers, they would have found another way to regain their magic and we might not have found out in time."

Dorothy continued her gentle sobbing as Princess Ozma continued soothing Her dear friend.

"Besides Dorothy, you thought only to show me your friendship and Love by way of these beautiful slippers, when all I ever really wanted was just your friendship and Love," the fairy princess proclaimed. Her gentle nature and soothing voice soon put a halt to Dorothy's tears and the young farm girl from Kansas slowly realized what her dearest friend in Oz had meant.

"Someday, when you are as old as I am, you'll come to understand that Love is the only gift that matters in this world... or any other," Princess Ozma explained, "and when you have Love, you have all you need."

Dorothy wondered once more how old Princess Ozma really was, but she knew from experience that her good friend was not about to confess that fact.

Besides, Uncle Henry had once told Dorothy that, "you never ask a lady how old she is, if you know what's good for you!"

Princess Ozma and Dorothy returned to the Great Hall and the celebrations and Dorothy felt much better about the whole thing.

She even managed a gentle laugh as she was joined by the Tin Woodman and the Scarecrow and all three of them watched as the Wizard of Oz danced a jig with Pacifico.

The Emerald Slippers of Oz

Later that day, Glinda, by means of her magic wand, sent 'Ol Mombi back to her old home in Gillikin Country, where the old woman's four-horned still waited for her return.

For 'Ol Mombi, the memories of the last few weeks had been wiped clean from her mind by the waters of the Forbidden Fountain and she fussed about her old home as though she had never left.

The Wizard of Oz delivered Dr. Pipt to his home by means of the old circus wagon and a rough climb up the rugged mountain where the former Crooked Magician and his wife lived. There, Margolotte, now awakened from her enchanted slumber, awaited his return.

"Where have you been?!" she shouted at her husband, who was quite bemused by his wife's reaction. "I've been here all alone for days, waiting on you to return from wherever you've been!"

Dr. Pipt was quite confused as his mind was also wiped clean of his adventures with magic.

"You haven't been playing with magic with that old magician, have you?!" she shouted once more, pointing at the Wizard of Oz, who only chuckled.

He knew it was folly to try and explain that when Dr. Pipt had attempted his spell of magic, it had actually worked, restoring Margolotte to her former self, though she too had no memory of the last few weeks.

The old magician left Dr. Pipt alone with Margolotte and laughed out loud as Dr. Pipt tried to explain to Margolotte that he "had no idea where he had been these last few weeks."

Blinkie found herself back at the old cave near her home in Jinxland where she had often ground plants and such into spices for her cooking. Standing before her was the old stone that she knew well. At her feet was a large pile of peppercorns, which the old woman began grinding into Pepperspice for her cooking needs. She didn't recall Dorothy using the Magic Belt to send her back home. For the old woman who once commanded all the witches of Jinxland, it was though she had never left home.

"I think I'll make me some Peppermint and Chamomile Tea when I'm done here," she mused to herself.

Chapter 41
Pacifico's Shop of Shoes

P rincess Dorothy swung the heavy wooden door open and walked softly into the old cobbler's shop. She was greeted by a lively, but short tune on a long golden horn that hung from a nearby hook upon the wall.

"Goodness!" she exclaimed. She laughed gently as Pacifico entered from the back room.

"Welcome, Princess Dorothy!" he said in greeting.

When Dorothy commented on the unique announcement of her arrival, Pacifico blushed.

"I didn't have the heart to dispose of the thing… and it does work well as a doorbell. I always know when I have a customer in the shop," he explained.

They both enjoyed a laugh and Pacifico offered Dorothy some tea and biscuits.

As they enjoyed themselves, Dorothy looked over the shop and noticed a small wooden perch in the corner by the workbench.

No sooner had she observed the perch when a grey

dove flew in from a nearby window and landed on the perch.

"Ugu!" shouted the little farm girl from Kansas.

The grey dove cooed joyfully.

"Now that the shop is mine, Ugu comes by every day to see that I'm making shoes the right way!" Pacifico explained. "He's still a great mentor, though I haven't quite figured out a way to make shoes that'll fit a bird's foot."

All three laughed at Pacifico's joke, then the grey dove flapped his wings a bit.

"As you can see, I'm happy to be a bird once more... and now I'm no longer lonely as I have my young apprentice to watch over," the grey dove explained.

Dorothy was very happy to see that Ugu had found happiness in his life as a grey dove.

"I have but one question, Princess Dorothy," Pacifico asked politely.

Dorothy wrinkled her nose and looked at Pacifico with kind eyes.

"I'll answer your question as best I can, but only if you don't call me Princess," she said kindly, but with great resolve.

Pacifico chuckled and agreed to Dorothy's request.

"If the Gemini Emeralds were magical, why didn't the spells the others cast work out like they had planned?" he asked. "I'm certain the spells they tried to cast were not nice at all, but instead, only pies, flowers and that funny horn came out of their attempt at magic?"

The Emerald Slippers of Oz

Dorothy nodded and leaned in to confide in both Pacifico and Ugu the Grey Dove.

"Few people know this, but emeralds in Oz are a magical gem which have been imbued with the power of Love. Queen Lurline Herself made it so long ago… "Dorothy whispered. "No matter how Evil the spell may be cast using any emerald in Oz, only good will come of that spell."

She could tell that Pacifico understood little of what she confided in him.

Ugu the Grey Dove however, understood exactly what Dorothy was saying. He knew full well from experience and was very grateful that his spell had not worked on Dorothy. The goodness that resulted from his spell was his return to his form as a bird, which he preferred.

"Only Dr. Pipt's spell worked, though only halfway," she continued on. "His love for his wife is what brought her back out of her enchanted sleep, but the rest of his spell only made flowers."

Pacifico nodded as though he understood… but he didn't understand, and was glad that he didn't.

For the bare-footed cobbler's apprentice with the blonde hair and gold ankle chain, there was no desire to do magic whatsoever… only to spend a lifetime making shoes for others.

For him, there would never be shoes on his bare feet.

As Dorothy made to return to Emerald City,

Pacifico cleared his throat and spoke up.

"Would you care for a pedicure and a nice coat of nail polish for your toenails, Miss Dorothy?" he announced. "It's my most popular request at the shop now... and everyone wants one!"

Princess Dorothy, Pacifico laughed loudly and at great length. Even Ugu joined in the merriment and before long, Dorothy had sat back down and removed her shoes for a nice, relaxing pedicure.

"Make mine a lovely emerald green color, if you please, master shoemaker!"